VIOLENT MEN

Hilt's fury comes from frustration. A nasty leg wound prevents him from resuming his hunt for the outlaw Buck Dunne. With his pursuit for the killer interrupted, Dunne will be long gone before Hilt can get his hands on him. But whilst Hilt believes that all the trouble in the county is over, unbeknownst to him, there are more rotten apples in the barrel with big trouble still imminent. A gun-crackling showdown with Buck Dunne is surely looming . . .

CORBA SUNMAN

VIOLENT MEN

Complete and Unabridged

LINFORD
Leicester

First published in Great Britain in 2011 by
Robert Hale Limited
London

First Linford Edition
published 2012
by arrangement with
Robert Hale Limited
London

British Library CIP Data

Sunman, Corba.
Violent men.- -(Linford western library)
1. Western stories.
2. Large type books.
I. Title II. Series
823.9′2–dc23

ISBN 978–1–4448–1277–0

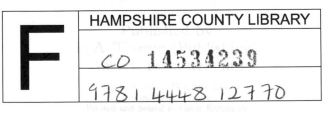
T. J. International Ltd., Padstow, Cornwall

This book is printed on acid-free paper

1

Hilt sighed for the hundredth time in as many minutes, and clenched his teeth as he involuntarily flexed his left arm and right leg in a ritual that was supposed to exercise them gently but punished him with a painful protest from his wounds as they stretched. But he was recovering slowly. He wiped sweat from his forehead as he leant back in the rocker on the porch of the Diamond O ranch in Texas and closed his eyes against the bleak scene that had become all too familiar over the past three weeks. His thoughts were in a rut — he could think of nothing but getting back on the trail of Buck Dunne, the outlaw who was responsible for the death of his brother, Thad Hilton. Impatience held him in its grip because, while he was lying up on this remote cow spread, Dunne, on the loose after

1

robbing the banks in Clarkville and Bitter Creek, was reported to be heading for the Mexican border.

Footsteps sounded on the porch at his side. Hilt looked up at the slight figure of Sue Ormond. His expression softened and he smiled. The sight of her keen blue eyes and the lovely lines of her face never failed to ease his disquiet, but he was saddened by the knowledge that his days here were coming to an end. Almost fit to ride, he was already chafing at the remaining time standing between him and his self-appointed chore of killing Buck Dunne. He had been hot on Dunne's trail when he was sidetracked by the trouble that had come to the Ormond family. They owned the Diamond O, and he had stopped over to help them out against the bad men intent on taking over their range.

'Having a good rest, Frank?' Sue enquired. She was tall and attractive, with a good figure and long blonde hair done up in a bun at the back of her shapely head. Her pale eyes were filled with concern as she looked at him, noting his disquiet and impatience.

'You know I can't rest while I'm aching for the day when I can hit Buck Dunne's trail,' he replied. 'I'm sorry, Sue, but that killer is getting further away while I'm sitting here doing nothing, and his trail will be cold by the time I am able to take out after him.'

'I understand,' Sue replied. 'I am aware that you'll leave us as soon as you can, and I'm dreading it. But I've promised myself that I'll be strong and not try to get you to change your mind. I know how you feel about hunting down that outlaw — blood is thicker than water. But will you promise to come back after you've settled your business with Dunne?'

'Sure.' Hilt nodded. 'That's if I'm still on my feet afterwards.'

He saw despair cross her lovely features and reached out with his right hand to grasp her wrist. The movement put a strain on his right thigh, and dull pain darted along the damaged nerves in the limb. He clenched his teeth until the spasm passed, aware that Sue was watching him closely.

'You're far from healed,' she observed. 'Try and be patient for a little longer. You'll never be able to sit a horse while your leg pains you.'

He nodded. His gaze travelled across the yard and he scanned the approaches to the ranch, lifting his right hand to shield his eyes against the glare of the sun. He stiffened when a moving speck on the town trail caught his intent gaze, and dropped his hand to the butt of the pistol nestling in the black leather holster on his cartridge belt lying on the arm of his chair.

'Someone's coming,' he said sharply. He drew the gun and checked it, then put it on his right knee and kept his hand on the butt.

'It's probably Billy.' Sue peered into the brassy sunlight. 'It's about time he got back from Cedar Creek. That brother of mine can't settle back to working on the ranch since the trouble. If he isn't hanging around you then he's riding off somewhere on his own. He doesn't seem to realize that the work of the ranch won't get done by itself.'

Hilt wiped sweat from his forehead. His gaze never left the approaching rider as the minutes passed.

'It isn't Billy,' he said at length.

'Maybe it is Doc Errol. He said he'd be out sometime to check on Pa and you.'

'It ain't the doc either.' Hilt observed.

'Well, it won't be Buck Dunne,' Sue retorted sharply.

'It is not Dunne I'm thinking about.' Hilt moistened his lips. 'There are men on my back trail who have been hunting me for months — kin to some of those men I've killed. They all want a shot at me for putting their folks into their graves. That's a harsh reality of my life, Sue. I've never murdered anyone — always given them a fair crack of the whip when the chips were down, even though some of them sneaked up on me intending to shoot me in the back because they were afraid to face me.'

'If you stayed here at the ranch they would soon forget about you,' Sue ventured.

Hilt shook his head. He watched the approaching rider, who was drawing close enough for details about him to become apparent.

'That's a stranger coming in,' he said. He grabbed his gun belt and pushed himself to his feet, ignoring the attendant pain in his leg. 'You'd better go inside the house and keep away from the windows,' he suggested. 'There might be shooting. I'll cross the yard, and that will stop any slugs coming your way.'

He buckled the cartridge belt around his slim waist, dropped his deadly right hand to the gun butt, and then slipped his injured left arm into the sling around his neck. He stifled a groan as he stepped down off the porch, and favoured his right leg considerably as he limped through the dust of the yard. He was tall and broad-shouldered, lean like a hunting dog, with brown eyes and black hair, and he was extremely fast with a gun. His gaze did not leave the approaching rider.

Hilt paused beside the well and stood with most of his weight on his left leg. When he glanced around at the porch he saw that Sue had gone back into the house. The rider passed beneath the high and wide gate and reined up before Hilt, who was resting his right hand on the butt of his holstered pistol.

'Howdy?' the man greeted. 'I'm Jay Wilson — looking for a riding job. I heard in town that you had some trouble here a month gone. I'd like to talk to Chuck Ormond.'

'Chuck is still in bed on account of the wound he collected in that trouble,' Hilt replied. 'His son Billy is running things until his pa can get back in harness, but Billy ain't here at the moment. You'll need to talk to him, Wilson, so come back later. There's no telling when Billy will show up.'

'It looks like you had your share of trouble. I saw you hobbling across the yard. But the trouble is over, so I heard.'

'It ain't for some folks.' Hilt became aware that the man's incisive gaze was subjecting the ranch to a close scrutiny while he talked, and he flexed the fingers of his right hand. He could read a man's intentions from his attitude, and alarm signals were flaring in his mind, although Wilson was sitting motionless on his horse and his right hand was not close to the pistol holstered on his right thigh. But Hilt could see tension in Wilson's gaze; a nervous energy being emitted unconsciously by his body, which radiated around him like an aura. Hilt had seen it many times before in the men who had confronted him, and he recognized it now.

'Mind if I get down and water my horse?' Wilson asked.

'Help yourself. Just don't make any sudden movement towards your gun because I'm still a mite hair-triggered after the trouble.'

Wilson nodded and dismounted. Hilt stepped backward a couple of paces when Wilson pushed the bucket into the well; the weight of it unwound the rope and there was a splash as the bucket hit the water below. Wilson peered into the well, checked that the bucket had submerged, and then turned the handle of the roller to bring it up out of the well, the creaking of the wooden roller as it turned breaking the even tenor of the heavy silence.

Sue screamed suddenly; a nerve-grating sound that tore through the brooding silence. Hilt jerked his head around and looked towards the house but caught Wilson's quick movement in the instant that he was distracted. Wilson released the handle and the bucket plummeted back into the well with a resounding splash. Wilson reached for his pistol; Hilt made a fast draw. Wilson's gun was already clearing his holster but Hilt beat him by a split second. Hilt's gun levelled, foresight covering Wilson's chest, and blasted raucously. Wilson was in the act of tilting his muzzle to line up on Hilt when the slug smacked into his chest. He yelled in agony, flung his arms wide and lost his grip on his gun as he was knocked backwards by the impact of the speeding bullet.

Hilt forgot about his healing wounds as he turned to the house. He ran across the yard with a kind of limping action in a desperate attempt to favour his right leg. He reached the porch as the front window was shattered on the inside by a bullet that breathed on the right side of his face in passing. Hilt hurled himself at the front door, which burst inwards, and blundered into the room, turning right towards the window. He saw Sue struggling in the grip of a stranger who was endeavouring to line up a pistol on Hilt's fast-moving figure.

Sue had both her hands around the man's gun wrist and was wrestling furiously to prevent him from firing the weapon. Hilt ignored the spasms of pain shooting through his arm and leg and hurtled into the fray. He reached around Sue and thrust the muzzle of his .45 against the side of the man's neck.

'Drop the gun,' Hilt commanded, 'or you're dead, mister.'

The man froze instantly. Sue released her grip and the man opened the fingers of his right hand. Sue grabbed his gun as he released it. She stepped back, cocking the weapon, and pointed it at the stranger, who raised his hands in token of surrender. Hilt was breathing heavily; his half-healed wounds racked him with pain. His pistol felt almost too heavy to hold but he steeled himself, gritting his teeth as he made the effort.

'He sneaked in the back door,' Sue gasped, her shoulders heaving. 'Where is the man who rode into the yard?'

'Dead, I should think,' Hilt replied. 'He pulled his gun when you screamed. It was a set-up. It looks like they reckoned to get me in a cross-fire.'

'Who are they?' Sue demanded.

'That is what I mean to find out.' Hilt turned his attention to the man. 'What's your name, buster, and what's your business?'

'I'm Pete Mitchell. Ask Wilson what it's all about. He got me into this.'

'Wilson is dead so I'm asking you.'

'You're Hilt, the gun fighter. You killed Wilson's uncle about six months ago on the Pecos, and we've been hunting you ever since. We heard a youngster in town bragging about the way you saved his ranch from thieves and we knew it was you from his description. We reckoned to catch you on the hop and finish you off.'

Hilt suppressed a sigh. Billy Ormond had gone too far with his hero worship; his loose tongue had brought about this shooting incident. He glanced at Sue, who was white-faced and shaking.

'I'll take this guy into town and have him jailed,' he said.

'But you're not fit to ride,' she protested.

'It looks like I've had all the rest I'm gonna get.' Hilt grimaced. 'It's time I moved on anyway, Sue. If I stay longer there will be others like these two coming in here to try and nail me. I'm too dangerous to have around, so don't try to talk me out of it. I know what I have to do. Anyway, Dunne is getting clear away while I'm lying up around here.'

He motioned with his gun and Mitchell stepped out to the porch. They crossed to the well. Wilson was lying on his back with his arms thrown wide. A large bloodstain covered his chest; his sightless eyes were open, staring up at the brassy sun. Sue followed them out of the house and stood in the background, still holding Mitchell's pistol, stricken by the turn of events.

'There's another rider coming in,' she said suddenly. Her tone was ragged and despair laced her voice.

Hilt caught the sound of hoofbeats

and glanced across the yard. 'It's Billy this time,' he observed.

Billy Ormond came into the yard at a canter. He reined up short when he saw the dead man lying in the dust.

'It looks like I'm too late!' Billy exclaimed, springing from his saddle. 'These two were asking questions about you in town, Hilt, and it wasn't until after they rode out that I got to figuring they might be planning to do you harm. I thought they were old friends of yours wanting to look you up.'

'Forget it,' Hilt said. 'Just remember that I don't have any friends. Saddle my horse for me, Billy, but get some rope first and hogtie this galoot. I'll drop him off at the jail in town before I shake the dust of this range off my boots. Throw Wilson back across his saddle and I'll take him to the undertaker.'

'You're not fit to ride yet,' Billy protested.

'I'll make out,' Hilt replied. 'Now get moving.'

'They've got a new sheriff in town,'

Billy said as he roped Mitchell's wrists together. 'His name is Ike Prescott.'

'Whoever he is, he'll be better than Catlin was,' Hilt mused. 'I'll hand Mitchell over to him. Did you hear anything of Buck Dunne around town?'

'Doc Errol said Dunne was spotted south of here a couple of days ago. He hit the bank over in Clarkville — killed a teller and a guard. They reckon he's heading for the border now. They say he's got away with four thousand dollars from his last two bank raids, and he'll likely go to ground until the dough runs out.'

Hilt turned to the house, and Sue accompanied him as he hobbled across the yard.

'I do wish you would change your mind about leaving,' she said. 'You know you won't help your wounds by travelling too soon.'

'I'd like to stay, but I'm certain it would be wrong. I can't risk anyone else sneaking in here, taking a shot at me and hitting you. Face up to it, Sue. You know it is time I was leaving. I've learned from experience never to stay too long in one place. If I hadn't stopped a couple of slugs I would have been long gone by now. You must realize that I don't choose to live this kind of life. It's what I've got, and I have to keep moving to stay alive.'

He went upstairs to his room, followed by Sue, and collected his gear. When he peered into Chuck Ormond's room he found Sue's father asleep. The rancher had been badly wounded in the recent trouble, but was on the mend.

'I won't wake him,' Hilt decided. 'He needs all the sleep he came get. I reckon he'll be on his feet again in another week.

'He'll be upset if you leave without seeing him,' Sue protested.

'I said I'll be coming back this way one day,' he replied with a smile.

'I'll count the hours until you do,' she responded.

Hilt led the way down to the porch. Billy was standing beside the two horses belonging to Mitchell and Wilson. Mitchell was upright in his saddle; tied hand and foot and looking dejected; Wilson was face-down across his saddle, blood dripping from his wound into the dust. Hilt's horse stood ready-saddled at the hitch rail in front of the porch.

'What will you do after you've been into town?' Sue asked.

Hilt shrugged. 'I'll try to pick up Dunne's trail,' he mused. 'If he was over in Clarkville a couple of days ago then I should be able to track him.'

'He's got a gang of around five men,' Billy said. 'Big odds, Hilt, and I reckon you'll need all the help you can get to face them.' He paused and then said hopefully, 'I'm at a loose end right now so why don't I tag along with you for a spell and kind of help you out?'

'There'll be plenty of help around if Dunne keeps hitting banks around here.' Hilt held out his hand. 'So long, Billy! Why don't you stick close to the ranch after this and settle down to what you were doing before I showed up? I know it's been a bad experience for you, but you're in the clear now.'

'I guess I owe it to you after what you did for us,' Billy replied. 'I'd like to ride with you, but I know you'd never let me do that; not in a hundred years. I hope you catch up with Dunne and kill him.'

'I'll do my best.' Hilt held out his hand to Sue but she pushed herself into his arms, her tears splashing his chin.

'I do wish you wouldn't go,' she said simply. 'You saved our lives, and you're not fit to ride yet. Another week or so wouldn't make much difference to your plans.'

'If I stayed another month I'd still have to ride out when the time comes, and it is better that I go now. With any luck I'll come up with Dunne pretty quick, and I promise that when I've put him down I'll come back.'

He disengaged himself from Sue and turned to his buckskin. He stifled a groan when he climbed awkwardly into the saddle; the wound in his leg protested sharply when he put his right foot into the stirrup. Billy tied the reins of the two horses together and slipped them over Hilt's saddle horn. Hilt shook his reins. The horse moved away, and Hilt sweated as the movement sent fresh agonies through his leg. He rode out of the yard, his teeth clenched. He kept his face averted from Sue and Billy to prevent them seeing the pain in his expression. To his relief, the pain eased slightly by the time he had reached the gate, and he glanced back to see Sue running into the house, her hands to her face.

Billy waved. Hilt responded, and then looked to his front and continued. He did not look back again. He glanced around instinctively, watching his surroundings from force of habit, attuning his mind to his usual high degree of alertness, and followed the trail to Cedar Creek.

It was just after noon when he topped a rise and saw two straggling rows of buildings facing each other along a short length of the trail. A large creek was off to the left, its smooth surface glittering in the sunlight. Cedar Creek looked sleepy in the brooding heat of the afternoon, but Hilt knew appearances could be deceptive. He thought of his first visit to this community, when he had shot Ben Hussey, the gambler, in the Black Ace saloon. Hussey had been fixing to kill Billy Ormond at the gaming table. Now Hussey was in jail, awaiting trial, and many other changes had been wrought during the trouble besetting the Diamond O ranch.

'What are you gonna do with me?' Pete Mitchell's harsh voice cut through the thread of Hilt's thoughts.

'Put you behind bars. You planned to kill me; you and Wilson. Do you reckon I should let you ride free?'

'You killed Wilson's uncle.'

'If I did then he must have asked for it. I always let the other feller make the first move. So if it was self defence then Wilson had no kick coming. His uncle got what he asked for.'

'They say you are looking for the outlaw Buck Dunne because he killed a brother of yours,' Mitchell persisted. 'So you know what it's like to feel the need to avenge kinfolk.'

'Wilson's uncle was no kin to you, huh? So why did you side Wilson?'

'He didn't think he could take you on his own. I wouldn't have shot you. I was with him for moral support, that's all. I'm not a killer. I've never shot a man.'

'And I don't figure to kill you,' Hilt replied. 'I'll hand you over to the law and let it deal with you.'

Hilt touched spurs to the buckskin and started down the long slope to the main street. Now he was impatient to shake the dust of this range off his boots. He had been sidetracked from his self-appointed chore of hunting Buck Dunne because he had stepped in to save Sue and her father from a couple of hard cases and became embroiled in the trouble that had erupted. But it was time to get back to his main purpose in life: hunting Dunne.

The livery barn was on the left as he entered Cedar Creek, and old John Ketchum, the liveryman, was leaning on a broom in the big open doorway of his barn.

'You found some more trouble, huh?' Ketchum demanded as Hilt rode by, leading the two horses.

'It was nothing I couldn't handle,' Hilt replied.

'I'd take a bet on that,' Ketchum replied. 'You sure altered the face of this community when you started in on the coyotes who figured to take over around here. Are these two part of the Catlin gang?'

'No.' Hilt shook his head. 'They crawled out of my past.'

He rode on, watching his surroundings as he traversed the street. A man appeared at the batwings of the Black Ace saloon, watched him pass without comment, and then followed along the sidewalk, his curiosity aroused. Hilt reined in at the hitch rail in front of the law office and gritted his teeth as he stepped down from his saddle. His left arm was filled with a dull ache and he could hardly bear to put weight on his right leg as he waited for his circulation to return to normal.

The door of the law office was opened abruptly and a tall, thickset man stepped into the doorway. He was wearing a law badge, and his right hand was down at his side, close to the butt of the Peacemaker in his holster. Hilt studied the man's craggy face.

'You'll be Ike Prescott, the new sheriff,' he remarked. 'The town will likely be a lot quieter than it was a month ago when I first rode in.'

'And who are you?' the sheriff demanded, 'riding in here with a dead man across his saddle, and a prisoner.'

'I'm Frank Blaine.' Hilt always used his mother's maiden name to conceal his identity. 'I've been out at Diamond O, resting up from a couple of wounds.'

'Frank Blaine. Heck, I've been

impatient to get out to the ranch to meet you. I heard what you did around here when the chips were down. You killed that crooked Sheriff Catlin!'

'And a few more of the rats that crawled out of the wood pile,' Hilt retorted.

'So who are these two? They sure made a big mistake picking on you. Bring your prisoner into the office and then give me the facts.'

Hilt turned to drag Mitchell out of his saddle. He glanced around the street from force of habit, and spotted several horses standing in front of the bank. A couple of men were on the sidewalk close to the front door of the bank and, even as Hilt registered the scene and felt a stab of suspicion, a gun was fired inside the building. The next instant the door was jerked open and three men emerged, carrying bulging saddle bags and waving pistols.

'The bank is being robbed!' Hilt shouted, reaching for his gun.

The sheriff reacted with impressive

speed. He stepped out of the office doorway, pulling his gun, but even so he was behind Hilt by a split second. The two men standing outside the bank began to shoot in their direction, and Hilt squeezed his trigger, aiming at the trio grabbing their horses. One thought was clear in his mind. This had to be a raid by Buck Dunne, and he meant to make the most of his luck.

2

Hilt ignored the slugs crackling around him as he triggered his deadly Colt. He saw a robber fall, heard Prescott's Colt blast into action, and looked more closely at the remaining men in front of the bank. He knew Buck Dunne by sight, having traded lead with him before in the hunt for his brother's killer. The meeting had proved inconclusive, but Hilt had retained a mental image of the outlaw. Dunne was a redhead; above average height, powerful and swaggering, with a moon face and a cruel mouth. His voice was loud; his tone insolent. He was an inveterate killer who liked to see men go down kicking with a slug in the guts.

A pang of disappointment stabbed through Hilt's chest when he failed to spot Dunne. A bullet tugged at the brim of his Stetson and brought his mind back to full alertness. He dropped to his left knee and pushed his right leg out at an angle to ease the throbbing pain in it. Two of the robbers swung into their saddles and whirled their horses away from the front of the bank. Prescott shot one off his animal, and the bag the man was holding in his left hand burst open when it hit the ground. Paper money flew on the breeze in a rich cascade. Hilt swung his Colt, following the progress of the second man, and, when he squeezed the trigger, the fleeing rider slumped forward over his saddle horn, clung to it for several paces, and then pitched sideways into the dust.

The harsh sound of the shooting boomed across the town and echoes fled. Several dogs started barking as silence returned. Hilt pushed himself upright. He looked over the scene of carnage in front of the bank as he reloaded his empty cylinder. Gun smoke was pungent in his nostrils. Five men were down in the dust. Prescott went forward, the sun glinting on the law badge pinned to his shirt. He grinned when he caught Hilt's eye.

'They sure didn't lie about you when they said you are hell on wheels,' he observed. 'Those robbers didn't have a chance. With you on the scene, their luck ran out in a big way. I could do with a man like you to be my chief deputy.'

Hilt grimaced and ignored the offer. 'When I saw what was happening I guessed this was Buck Dunne's gang,' he replied. 'But I didn't see him around.'

'Do you know Dunne by sight?' Prescott asked. 'I've got his face on a dodger, and eye witness reports have pinned the recent robberies at Bitter Creek and Clarkville on him. He's been real busy around here.'

'I've been on his trail for months,' Hilt admitted. 'He killed my brother.'

Hilt held his gun in his hand as they approached the fallen men. Three of the robbers were dead; two were still breathing.

Townsfolk were emerging from the buildings fronting the street. Prescott shouted to one of them to fetch the doctor. Hilt looked into the faces of the robbers, and was disappointed that Dunne was not one of them. He was aware that his life would have become easier if the outlaw had been down in the dust. But he could not accept that this was not Dunne's gang. There couldn't be two gangs of bank robbers operating in the same area.

Prescott and some of the townsmen scurried around picking up the money that was strewn along the street. Hilt entered the bank to find a bank clerk dead on the floor and a man sitting at a desk holding a hand pressed to his left shoulder with blood dribbling between his fingers. A back door stood open, and Hilt regarded it curiously. He turned to the man at the desk.

'Did any of the robbers leave by the back door?' he demanded.

'Two did,' the man gasped. 'They

came in that way and took us by surprise.'

Hilt limped to the door, passed through a small back room, and went out to the back lots. His teeth clicked together when he saw two riders galloping away into the distance. He watched them for a moment but was unable to make out details. He limped back into the bank.

'Describe the two who got away,' he suggested. 'Was one of them a big redhead?'

'I'm James Leat; I own the bank. Get Doc Errol in here to stop me bleeding and then I'll talk to you.'

'Prescott has sent for the doc,' Hilt replied. 'He'll be in here presently. Your money is safe. We happened to be standing outside the law office when the robbers took off, and none of them out front got away. Now tell me about the two who made it out the back door. I need to know if one of them was Buck Dunne.'

'Dunne was one of them.' Leat spoke

through clenched teeth. His fleshy face was pale and shock showed plainly in his dark eyes. 'I've seen a wanted poster of him. He has got red hair, and he's a real tough killer. Is Tom Fallon dead?' He glanced at the man lying on the floor. 'Dunne didn't have to shoot him. We did not attempt to hinder him. Dunne shot Tom down in cold blood and then turned his gun on me.'

'That's the way Dunne operates. I'll send the doc into you as soon as he shows up.' Hilt went out to the sidewalk. He saw the tall, thin figure of Doc Errol coming along the sidewalk and beckoned him, then pointed into the bank.

'The banker needs your help, Doc,' he called.

Doc Errol glanced at the fallen robbers as he passed them. 'Looks like two of these require my services,' he observed. 'Is Leat seriously hurt?'

'You'd better attend to him first. He's got a shoulder wound. The teller is dead.' Hilt turned to Prescott, who was still picking up loose money. 'Buck Dunne got away out back,' he announced. 'I'm taking out after him. I haven't been this close to him in a couple of months.'

'I'll get a posse together and follow you as soon as I can,' Prescott said.

Hilt went to his horse and swung gingerly into the saddle. His leg was protesting at the rough treatment it had received and he had never felt less like riding, but nothing was more important than getting Dunne. He rode into an alley beside the bank and paused on the back lot. He could see where two horses had stood while the bank raid had taken place, and examined their tracks without dismounting. Hoof prints were deep and plain in the dust: the trail was perfectly clear. He touched spurs to his buckskin and set out in pursuit, his aches and pains pushed into the background of his mind. The hunt was on again, and this time nothing would distract him from the grim task of hunting down his brother's killer.

The two sets of tracks headed south.

Hilt followed them intently, mindful of the fact that Dunne would probably lie up once clear of town to wait for any survivors of his gang and to check on the degree of pursuit that would evolve. The gang had hit three banks in the area in recent weeks, and it was likely that the rumours of Dunne making for the Mexican border were true. Hilt was determined to catch the outlaw before he could escape justice.

But it did not take Hilt long to realize that he was not up to the chase. Despite his dedication, his aches and pains filled the forefront of his mind, and before he had ridden a mile he had to stop and dismount. The wound in his right thigh was throbbing intolerably. He stood with his foot raised from the ground in an effort to ease the pain; galled by the bitter knowledge that he could not ride on.

He gazed at the two sets of tracks, frustrated by the situation. It was ironic that his best chance of catching Dunne should turn up when he was physically unable to follow the outlaw's trail. He clung to his saddle horn, stretched his leg out stiffly, and swung it gently in an attempt to alleviate the pain. He was still standing irresolute when the sound of several horses on his back trail alerted him and he turned to see Sheriff Prescott and three townsmen approaching.

Prescott reined in, reading the situation at a glance. Hilt sighed heavily as he pointed to the tracks left by Dunne and his companion.

'Dunne is all yours, Sheriff,' he said in a low tone. 'I can't ride another inch. I hope you get him.'

Prescott nodded. 'You'd better head back to town. I'll see you when I get back. Come on, men, let's get after Dunne. I want to nail him before sundown.'

The posse rode on and Hilt watched them until they were out of sight. He turned his horse to face the distant town and began to limp towards it, finding it easier to walk than to sit his jolting saddle, but after fifty yards he had to halt again, and leaned on his saddle with only the toe of his right boot on the ground and most of his weight on his uninjured limb. He could see the town clearly, and shook his head as he gazed at it, aware that he should have listened to Sue's advice when he had had the chance. He trailed his reins and the buckskin took the opportunity to crop the bunch grass while he lowered himself to the ground and stretched out on his back in an attempt to find easement from his pain.

Hilt closed his eyes, resigned to the frustrating situation. As the minutes passed his pain subsided slightly and he hoped it would fade completely. He was contemplating rising to continue when he caught the sound of approaching hoofs and heard a wagon creaking. He sat up and looked around. A buckboard was coming across the range from the west to join the trail to town. Hilt grasped his reins and caught hold of a stirrup. He hauled himself to his feet and stood watching the wagon, which was being driven by a whiskered old man who hauled on his reins and brought his team to a halt beside Hilt.

'Have you got trouble, mister?' the oldster demanded.

Hilt explained tersely, and saw suspicion fade out of the man's narrowed eyes.

'So you're the guy who helped Chuck Ormond out of his bad business, huh? Say, I'm mighty glad to make your acquaintance. There's been nothing but talk about you for the past month. I'm Bill Dixon, cook at the Flying W. I'm heading into town for provisions, so hitch your horse to the wagon and climb in back.'

'Thanks, Bill.' Hilt did not need a second invitation, and sighed with relief when he was stretched out on some empty sacks on the floor of the buckboard. Dixon cracked his whip and the vehicle moved on. Hilt gritted his teeth as the wheels grated over the uneven trail, and gripped his right thigh with both hands in an attempt to ease the pain; grimly aware that riding a wagon was easier than sitting a horse.

There was no evidence of the bank raid in the main street when the wagon stopped outside the general store. The bodies of the robbers had been removed and their horses were gone, but a crowd of townsfolk thronged the wide thoroughfare and excitement seemed to crackle in the air as the raid was discussed. Hilt eased himself out of the wagon and dusted himself down. A tall young man wearing a deputy sheriff badge pinned to his shirt front stepped out of the crowd and confronted Hilt.

'I'm John Fletcher,' he introduced. 'Did you lose Dunne's trail? Is the sheriff following Dunne?'

Doc Errol approached as Hilt explained the situation. The deputy turned away after listening, and Errol placed a hand on Hilt's shoulder.

'Are you planning on returning to the Diamond O until you are fit to ride on?' Errol enquired.

Hilt shook his head. 'No, Doc, but

I've curbed my impatience. I tried to follow Dunne but it is more than flesh and blood can manage. I've said my goodbyes to Sue and Billy Ormond so I'll stick around town until I can ride again.'

'You can stay at my house until you're fit,' Errol said, 'and I'll be able to keep an eye on your wounds. This county owes you a big debt, and I'd like the chance to repay some of it. Why don't you come with me now and let me check on your leg? I reckon you could have put yourself back by as much as a week by trying to take up the trail too soon.'

'I'm inclined to agree with you,' Hilt said. 'Sue advised me to lie up longer but I'm kind of bull-headed when it comes to Dunne, and I wasted some time fighting the trouble you had around here. But impatience won't help, and I'm resigned to the situation now.'

He led his buckskin and limped beside the doctor to his house.

'Leave your horse outside,' Errol suggested. 'I've got a barn out back where I keep my horse, and your buckskin can share it.'

Hilt nodded and wrapped his reins around a rail. He followed the doctor into the house and they entered the office. Errol checked Hilt's left arm, and grimaced when he had exposed the wound.

'You haven't done yourself any favours by trying to move out too soon,' Errol observed, 'and I suspect your thigh will be even worse than your arm. Drop your pants and I'll take a look at the leg.'

Hilt obeyed, and Errol shook his head. 'The thigh is badly inflamed. You're going to have to treat it with great care or complications might set in. If that happens you could lose the leg.'

'Are you joshing me?' Hilt demanded.

'No. That's not in my line of business. I'm giving you the plain, unvarnished truth. Rest up completely for at least a week or you'll be in real trouble.'

'Sure thing, Doc, I get the message.' Hilt nodded.

'You don't have to go to bed,' Errol pointed out. 'I'll fix you up so you can sit with your leg outstretched, and all you'll have to do is rest. Give yourself a week. Leave the man-hunting to Ike Prescott. He seems to know what he is doing. Take my advice and you'll be riding out this time next week. Dunne's trail will still be there — if Prescott doesn't catch him first.'

Hilt nodded. He had learned his lesson, and made no fuss when Errol installed him in the living room in an easy chair with a cushioned footstool under his leg.

'It is going to be a long week,' Hilt prophesied, and sighed heavily as he resigned himself to the situation.

★　★　★

As he made his escape across the back lots, Buck Dunne was concerned by the volume of shooting he had heard from

40

the front of the bank. He kept glancing along his back trail, and was not reassured when he saw no sign of pursuit. His pale eyes glinted while his agile mind thrust up reasons why his gang had not rejoined him, but he sensed that they had been shot down, and when he reached the first crest on the trail south he reined in and swung out of his saddle. Tall and powerfully built, he pushed back his Stetson to reveal reddish hair; there was a straggly red growth on his face. His pale green eyes held a disconcerting belligerence in their glassy depths and there was a cruel twist to his thin-lipped mouth.

His companion, Hoagy Benton, a tall, thin, dark-skinned outlaw who looked as if he had not washed in three months, did not dismount but sat his horse with hunched shoulders; his brown eyes were unblinking as he watched their back trail.

'What in hell do you reckon happened to the rest of the gang, Buck?' Benton demanded without taking his gaze off the trail. 'Their orders were to ride out when you fired a shot inside the bank. Why ain't they done like you said?'

'You must have heard all that shooting out front as we pulled out,' Dunne rasped in a brittle tone. 'There's a new sheriff in Cedar Creek, and I reckon he showed up just when we didn't need him around. The last time I saw Catlin he said there was some bad trouble around here, and the town is still het up about it. That's how come we got trouble when we hit the bank.'

'But most of the dough went out the front door with the gang,' Benton complained. 'It is a good thing I kept hold of one sack or we'd be empty-handed. We oughta ride back there to see what's doing. We might be able to pick up some more of the dough.'

'I've got a better idea,' Dunne said. 'Leave that sack of dough with me and you ride back into town to see what's happened. I'll wait here for you. If some of the boys are behind bars then we'll have to bust them out.'

'OK.' Benton nodded. 'I ain't on the wanted list like you.' He tossed the bulging canvas bag to Dunne, who caught it deftly. He set spurs to his mount, but then reined in quickly. 'Hey, Buck,' he said. 'There are four riders heading this way.'

Dunne had already spotted the group coming resolutely along his back trail. He fixed the money bag to his saddle horn.

'We'd better get outa here,' he rasped. 'That looks like a posse.'

'It would be better to stop them cold.' Benton snatched his Winchester from its boot. 'If they start chasing us they'll never give up, and my horse is about played out. Let us put them down in the dust.'

'Sure!' Dunne reached for his rifle. 'That guy in the lead is wearing a law badge. It must be that new sheriff we heard about. It's a pity Catlin was killed. We knew where we were with him in the law saddle, even if he did want a big percentage of our takings.'

'And Chain Toll, the deputy, was killed as well. There ain't anyone on the side of the law that we can trust any more. Things are coming to a bad pass, Buck. It's about time we cleared out of this county and headed for some place that's quieter.'

Dunne led his horse halfway down the reverse slope, trailed his reins, and then moved back to the crest. He dropped into cover and Benton joined him. They watched the four riders approaching, obviously following tracks. Dunne jacked a cartridge into the breech of his rifle; Benton did likewise. They waited patiently for the posse to ride into range.

Ike Prescott studied the ground ahead with an experienced eye. He expected the outlaws to stop and check for pursuit, and he surveyed the crest before them as they reached rising ground. He saw nothing suspicious until sunlight glinted on Benton's rifle as the outlaw loaded it.

'Take cover,' Prescott yelled, diving

out of his saddle. He hit the ground and rolled into a depression, snaking his pistol out of its holster as he did so and covering the crest. ✕

The three posse men vacated their saddles, and were hunting cover when two rifles on the crest cut loose at them. Joe Fenton, a local carpenter, was hit in the chest by Dunne's first shot. He felt no pain as he fell on his face — the rifle slug pierced his heart and he never knew what hit him. Dunne swung his rifle to cover the spot where the sheriff had gone to ground. He saw Benton's shots striking around the positions taken up by the other two posse men.

Prescott raised his head cautiously, pistol ready to return fire. Sweat was running into his eyes as he endeavoured to locate the positions of the outlaws. Dunne aimed at the sheriff's black Stetson, and when he fired, his bullet struck the hat just above its leather band; it smacked into Prescott's skull, and sent the hat and most of the sheriff's brains flying. The two posse men ducked and stayed low while Dunne and Benton amused themselves with an occasional shot to keep them pinned down.

Pete Drew, another of the posse men, who spent his nights working in the saloon as an assistant bartender, jumped up from his cover and made a dash for his horse, which had turned back down the slope when he vacated the saddle. He took four quick paces before Dunne shot him in the back. When Drew fell lifeless, Dan Maxwell, who worked for Pierce, the undertaker, lifted his pistol and emptied it at the crest. He ducked to reload, and then emptied the gun again in a desperate spate of wild shooting. Dunne ducked a lucky shot which tore through the brim of his Stetson, and then eased back from the crest.

'I'm gonna pull out, Hoagy.' he rasped. 'When that last posse man lights out for town you follow him in and learn what you can about the situation. See Vince Parker, who owns the Black Ace saloon — he's a good pard of mine — and ask around about a guy who showed up some weeks ago saying he was trailing me. Catlin told me about him — said his name is Frank Blaine — I was supposed to have killed his brother. He was the one making all the trouble for Catlin. He holed up on the Diamond O ranch and shot the hell out of the bunch who was trying to take over around here. See what you can find out about him, huh? I've got an urge to wait for you at Diamond O. I think I'll ride over there now and settle in. We'll lie up there for a few days before hitting the bank in Cedar Creek again, and then we'll head on into Mexico.'

'OK, boss.' Benton peered down the slope. 'Do you want me to plug the guy looking for you, if I see him?'

'No. I'll catch up with him later. I've got a feeling he'll be at the Diamond O. I'll scout out the place before I move in, and I might just catch him cold. Do like I tell you — don't foul up. When you're through in town you can come out to the ranch.'

Dunne rode away. Benton listened to his departure but did not take his eyes off the surviving posse man's position. When Maxwell jumped up out of cover and ran down the slope, Benton held his fire. Maxwell threw himself into his saddle and rode hell for leather back in the direction of the town. Benton waited thirty minutes before fetching his horse, and then rode down the slope to rob the dead posse men. He took a gold pocket watch and a sheaf of folding money from the sheriff before making a wide detour to get to Cedar Creek from a different direction . . .

3

The posse man, Pete Maxwell, raised dust back to town and hit the main street at a gallop. He reined in at the rail in front of Doc Errol's house and sprang from his saddle. Errol came to his door when Maxwell hammered on it, and grabbed his medical bag when he heard the details of the ambush.

'My horse is in the barn out back, Pete,' Errol said. 'Saddle it for me, will you? I need to talk to a patient before I can ride with you.'

'Sure, Doc.' Maxwell dashed sweat from his face. 'I don't reckon there is any hurry. It looked like the sheriff and the others were dead.'

Errol went into the room where Hilt was resting and gave him the news of the ambush. Hilt made as if to get up but changed his mind. He leaned back and shook his head helplessly.

'I guess there is nothing I can do if Prescott is dead,' he mused. 'This damned leg! It wouldn't be so bad if I could get around on it.'

'There's no chance of that.' Errol shook his head. 'I'm riding out to the ambush spot now. I'll have a wagon sent out from the livery barn to collect the bodies.'

'I sure wish I could ride out on Dunne's trail,' Hilt groaned.

'The only thing you can do is rest up to aid your recovery,' Errol insisted. 'You'll have your chance of getting Dunne later. I'll see you when I get back.'

Hilt moved uneasily in his seat as the doctor departed. A few moments later he heard the sound of hoofs pounding away along the street. He put his right leg down on the floor and tried to stand up to test it, but raw pain stabbed through the limb and he clenched his teeth as he lifted his foot back on to the stool. The pain lessened again, and he sat thinking about the ambush, aware that the sheriff and his posse would still be alive if he had been fit to chase after Dunne as he had planned.

Doc Ellis was gone almost two hours, and when he returned to his house he found Hilt consumed by impatience. The doctor's face was grim; he shook his head at the silent question showing in Hilt's expression.

'They are all dead,' Errol said. 'Ike Prescott was shot through the head, and the two posse men were gunned down. There was no sign of Dunne and his companion — Pete Maxwell said there were two ambushers. I looked around for their tracks leading away from the scene of the ambush and found that they rode off in different directions. They've split up, Hilt, and there is no telling which one was Dunne or where he went. I've instructed John Ketchum, the liveryman, to take a buckboard out and pick up the three bodies.'

'I'd soon get on Dunne's trail if I could get out there for a look around,' Hilt said. 'My leg ain't too bad if I can keep my weight off it. It's standing on it that's causing the problem.'

Errol put a hand on Hilt's arm. 'Say, I might be able to help you with that,' he mused. 'Hold on a moment.'

The doctor left the room and went into his office, to return a moment later carrying a wooden crutch.

'Try this for size,' he said. 'Put the padded end in your right armpit and take hold of the horizontal bar. Lean your weight on the crutch and raise your foot off the ground.' He nodded when Hilt obeyed his instructions. 'It looks like it'll be just right for you,' he observed. 'You should be able to keep your foot up off the ground, and practice will have you moving around with no difficulty.'

Hilt leaned on the crutch with the thick pad in his right armpit. His right hand rested comfortably on the short horizontal bar. He took a couple of experimental steps and discovered that when his right foot was held clear of the ground he was not troubled by the agonizing pain which gripped him when the limb was taking his weight.

'This is all right, Doc,' he said joyfully. 'Why didn't you think of this before? But I still can't sit on a horse.'

'I've got a buggy out back which I use occasionally,' Errol said. 'You could borrow that so long as you leave your horse here for me to use.'

'What are we waiting for?' Hilt lurched towards the door and Errol hurried to open it for him.

They went through to the back of the house and Errol led the way out to his barn. Hilt stood leaning on the crutch while Errol harnessed a brown mare and hitched her to the buggy. When Hilt climbed into the vehicle he stretched out his right leg. Errol studied him for a moment, then fetched a gunny sack, stuffed it with straw and placed it on the floor of the buggy.

'Rest your right foot on the sack and see how it feels,' Errol advised.

Hilt obeyed, and then nodded. 'It's OK,' he said. 'I'll give it a try. I'll need my rifle, Doc, and my saddle-bags off the buckskin.'

'Drive round to the front of the house and we'll set you up,' Errol replied.

Hilt was filled with relief by the time he was ready to take the trail. He shook the reins and the mare set off obediently with a smooth running stride that covered the ground swiftly. Hilt left town and sent the mare along the tracks left by the posse. When he reached the spot there was plenty of evidence to show exactly where the ambush had taken place. Hilt climbed out of the buggy and used the crutch to move around. He saw Ike Prescott stiffening under the hot sun, his head shattered by a .44–.40 rifle slug, and two of the posse men were stretched out in careless attitudes of death.

He was able to read the sequence of the action from the tracks on the slope, and worked his way up to the crest. He found the spot where the two outlaws had lain in wait for the posse to draw within range — several empty cartridge cases glinted in the sunlight. Hilt moved around, relieved that he was getting hardly any discomfort from his leg. He moved on to the spot where two horses had stood in cover on the reverse slope while the deadly ambush took place. He studied the tracks of the horses and noted that one set went down the slope back to where the sheriff was lying while the other headed off on a circuitous route apparently to bypass Cedar Creek.

Hilt went back down the slope to study the tracks left by the rider who had returned to the fallen sheriff. He noted that the rider had dismounted and stood beside Prescott. Hilt bent over the lawman to search his pockets, and his eyes took on a bleak expression when he discovered them empty; he recalled noticing that Prescott had been wearing a gold watch chain, which was now missing. He went on to study the tracks the outlaw had made after quitting the scene, and judged that they were heading back to town.

He climbed into the buggy and returned to where the two horses had waited on the reverse slope. The outlaw departing in the other direction had ridden east. Hilt spent some minutes studying the prints of both horses, memorizing them for future reference. He did not think Dunne would ride back into Cedar Creek because his face was too well known. He leaned on the crutch and looked towards the town: a buckboard was approaching, accompanied by a rider.

Hilt went back to the buggy and drove to meet the buckboard. He recognized the liveryman, John Ketchum, who was driving the creaking vehicle, and the escorting rider looked familiar.

'Howdy,' Hilt greeted. He looked intently at the rider. 'You were with the sheriff earlier, weren't you?'

Pete Maxwell nodded. His face was pale and he was clearly shocked. 'I was with the posse. We never had a chance. Two of those outlaws were on the crest and they cut loose at us without warning. When the posse and the sheriff were killed, I headed back to town.'

'Did you get a look at either of the outlaws?' Hilt asked.

Maxwell shook his head. 'No chance,' he said. 'They poured slugs into us. The shooting was so fierce I don't know how they missed me.'

'I've looked at tracks on the crest,' Hilt mused. 'One of the outlaws went down to the posse after you pulled out, and it looks like he robbed them. The sheriff's pockets were rifled — everything taken, and I recall seeing a watch chain going into the breast pocket of his jacket when I spoke to him earlier.'

'Ike was real proud of that watch,' Maxwell said. 'He was presented with it by the folks of San Antone, where he was in the law department for several years.'

'I'll check out Cedar Creek for the outlaw that went back there,' Hilt mused. 'I might be able to drop on to him. He'll be a stranger, which will help. I do know Buck Dunne by sight, but I don't think he would risk showing his face in town, so I'll check out the second trail of prints after I've looked around.'

'I'll go with you when I've helped load the bodies on the buckboard,' Maxwell said. 'I'd like to come face to face with either of those two who ambushed us.'

'I haven't a legal right to do anything about this business,' Hilt observed, 'but I can't stand by after what happened today. I'll go on to town. You can catch up with me when you've finished here.'

Maxwell nodded. Hilt shook the reins and set the mare into motion. He checked his pistol as he drove back to town. His thoughts turned over the situation, and he hoped that Dunne had made a mistake and returned to Cedar Creek instead of riding clear, but he was not optimistic. Pete Maxwell caught him up as he entered the main street. Hilt reined in at the doctor's house, and Errol emerged from the building. The doctor listened to Hilt's report.

'I'll get my gun and accompany you,' Errol said. 'I'll keep an eye on the law department until another sheriff is appointed, although I don't know where another good man will be found. The new deputy, John Fletcher, has quit and pulled out so I'll handle the law for the time being. We'll need to search the town for a stranger. Are you sure one of the outlaws came back here?'

'I kept an eye on his tracks all the way from the ambush site,' Hilt said. 'He came into town, all right, and if we don't find him inside of town limits I'll check the other side of town to see if he rode on through.'

Errol nodded. 'You seem to know what you are doing. How's the leg holding up?'

'It's in pretty good shape so far. The crutch is doing the trick.' Hilt glanced around the street. 'Pete, why don't you go along to the livery barn and check for a stranger's horse? If you find one, or see anyone suspicious, don't try anything by yourself. Come for me and I'll handle him.'

Maxwell touched spurs to his mount and set off along the street. Doc Errol went into his house to emerge a moment later stuffing a pistol into the waistband of his pants. He climbed into the buggy beside Hilt.

'Drive as far as the saloon,' he suggested. 'Most men, when they hit town, drop in there for a drink. Vince Parker runs the Black Ace saloon, and he'll know if there are any strangers around.'

Hilt drove to the saloon and they alighted. Hilt used the crutch, and checked that he could reach the butt of his pistol while the crutch was in place under his armpit. Satisfied that he would not be inconvenienced, he followed Errol into the saloon. He glanced around: the saloon was deserted, except for a bartender polishing the top of the bar. Errol walked to the bar with silent steps, and Hilt thumped the floorboards with the crutch.

'Howdy, Doc?' The bartender greeted. 'What'll it be, gents?'

'Hello, Jack. Rye for me,' Errol replied. 'I could do with something strong. What about you, Hilt?'

'Beer,' Hilt responded.

Doc glanced around. 'Place looks like a ghost town,' he observed.

'I have been busy,' the tender said. 'We were busting at the seams after the bank raid. I reckon everyone has gone home now to eat. Wait until the word gets out that Ike Prescott has been killed.'

'Word gets around pretty fast.' Errol commented. 'Who told you about the sheriff?'

'There was a stranger in here about fifteen minutes ago — said he saw three bodies lying on a slope two miles south of town, and one of them was wearing a law badge.'

'Where is the stranger now?' Hilt asked.

'He had a beer and then wanted the

61

restaurant. I sent him along to Dan's place.'

'What does he look like?' Hilt persisted.

'Like a long rider.' The bartender grimaced. 'He's a tall, thin feller; wearing a dirty blue shirt, scuffed black boots, and has half a dozen pistol cartridges stuck in the hatband of his black Stetson. It's funny, but you don't see that kind of thing very often these days. He had a smell of gun smoke about him — his clothes reeked of it. That was the first thing I noticed about him.'

'Drink up, Hilt, and we'll check him out,' Errol said.

They gulped their drinks, left the saloon and went to the restaurant, which was crowded. Hilt spotted a man wearing a blue shirt sitting alone at a corner table. He was eating a big steak and a pile of boiled potatoes. A Stetson was lying on the table, and Hilt noticed several cartridges stuffed inside the hatband.

'Leave this to me, Doc,' Hilt said. 'We don't want any trouble in here.'

'You want to wait until he leaves?' Errol demanded.

'No. I need to get after Buck Dunne as soon as I can, and if this guy is one of the bank robbers then the other outlaw, who rode off east from the ambush spot, will be Dunne himself. I don't want to waste any more time, Doc. I'll take this guy real quiet and see what he can tell us.'

Errol sat down at a table near the door and Hilt picked his way between the small tables to where the man wearing the blue shirt was seated.

'Mind if I sit here?' Hilt asked.

Hoagy Benton looked up and his mouth stopped chewing; gravy ran down his chin and he wiped it off with the cuff of his left sleeve. He glanced around before nodding. 'It's OK by me,' he replied. He glanced at Hilt's crutch and grimaced. 'So what happened to you? Fall off your horse?'

'No.' Hilt dropped into a vacant seat.

Benton stuffed a piece of beef into his mouth. Hilt leaned closer, caught the pungent smell of gun smoke clinging to his clothes, and reached for his holstered gun. Benton caught the slick movement and looked up from his plate. His jaw dropped when he saw the muzzle of Hilt's Colt peering at him over the edge of the table. Food fell from his gaping mouth, which he closed quickly. Then he froze.

'You've got the right idea,' said Hilt. 'Put both your hands on the table top, and don't even blink. I'll relieve you of your gun and then we'll take a walk.'

'What the hell!' Benton spoke hoarsely. 'What gives? You ain't wearing a law badge. What is this — a hold up?'

'No. I heard you found the spot where an ambush took place earlier. You told the bartender in the Black Ace saloon that you saw the sheriff and two posse men lying dead out on the range.'

'That's right; so what?'

'So we'll go somewhere quiet and talk about it. Do like I say and you won't get hurt.'

'The hell I will! I'm gonna finish my

steak before I get off this seat.'

'You could die sitting there,' said Hilt. He lifted his pistol clear of the table and cocked it.

Benton's eyes narrowed. He stared at the gun as if he had never seen one before. He moistened his lips. Hilt could almost see his brain working.

'OK,' Benton said at length. 'I don't know what your game is, but I'll go along with it. I ain't done anything wrong. All I did was happen on a spot where an ambush took place. I heard shooting before I got to it, and there was no one around when I found the bodies. I noticed one of them was wearing a sheriff star. That's all I can tell you. There's no need to drag me outa here. Let me finish my steak.'

'What's your name,' demanded Hilt.

'I'm Hoagy Benton.'

'Where is Buck Dunne heading? You two split up after shooting the posse that chased you out of town after you robbed the bank this morning.'

'Hey, you're getting me mixed up

with someone else! I don't know anything about robbing a bank. And who is Buck Dunne? I never heard of the guy. I've been on the trail for three days. I came straight from Rimrock, west of here. I was working there for a trader name of Monte Grand.'

'Ike Prescott, the sheriff, had a watch on him this morning. When his body was picked up, the watch was missing. Turn out your pockets.'

Benton started his right hand towards the edge of the table in the direction of his holstered pistol, but thought better of it. He halted the movement. His expression hardened and he leaned back in his seat.

'OK, I took the watch,' he admitted. 'I also took a few dollars for eating money. Anyone would have done that, finding them bodies like I did. You can have the watch back.'

'Sure. So where is your horse?'

'What's my horse got to do with it?' Benton forced a grin. 'You don't think he set the ambush, do you?'

'I checked out the ambush,' Hilt said patiently, 'and noted the prints left by the two horses the ambushers rode out of there. If your horse didn't leave one of those sets of tracks then I guess you're telling the truth. So let's go and check, huh?'

The fingers of Benton's right hand twitched, and Hilt noted the reaction.

'Get your hands up above your shoulders,' ordered Hilt. 'Don't make any mistakes now. I'll take your gun. Then we'll sort this out peaceably.'

Benton heaved a sigh and put his hands up. Hilt got to his feet, his gun steady. He stood over Benton and used his left hand to snake the man's pistol from its holster.

'Now get up and make for the door,' commanded Hilt.

Benton shrugged, but obeyed reluctantly. Doc Errol opened the street door and they left the restaurant. Benton paused on the sidewalk and looked around the street. Hilt pushed him in the back to get him moving.

'Where is Dunne?' demanded Hilt.

'You're talking about someone I don't know,' said Benton.

'We'll see.' Hilt leaned his weight on the crutch and kept his right foot off the ground. 'Where is your horse, mister?'

'I left him on the back lot behind the saloon.'

'Why didn't you stable it like any normal man would have done?' Doc Errol spoke in a low tone. 'You look like a bank robber to me. Why did you come back to town?'

'I've never been in this burg before! How many times do I have to tell you? So I came upon an ambush spot! Big deal!'

'Lead the way to where you left your horse,' said Hilt. 'And I want to know how come you smell of gun smoke. Your clothes reek of it. I'm betting you were involved in the ambush. Why don't you tell us what is going on? Buck Dunne is wanted by the law — there's a price on his head.'

Benton stifled a sigh and entered a nearby alley.

Doc Errol kept his pistol in his hand as they walked to the back lots. Hilt transferred his Colt to his left hand. They approached a bay horse that was standing hipshot, its reins wrapped around a post.

'Keep him covered, Doc,' said Hilt. He stumped around the horse, looking closely at the dust and staying clear of the prints the animal had made. After studying the tracks intently, he looked up at the sullen Benton.

'You're one of the men who laid that ambush,' said Hilt. 'I memorised the two sets of tracks, and this horse made one of them. You'll come clean if you know what's good for you, Benton. The men hereabouts will likely want to do something about you for killing their sheriff. I reckon there will be only Doc and me standing between you and a lynch rope. So tell us what happened and where Dunne has gone, and we'll see that you get a fair trial.'

'I've got nothing to say.' Benton spoke through stiff lips. His expression was sullen. 'I keep telling you the truth but you won't believe me, so I'll keep my mouth shut.'

Hilt glanced at Doc Errol, saw that he was covering Benton with his pistol, and holstered his gun in order to free his hands. The crutch was cumbersome to handle, and he motioned for Benton to step away from the horse before opening the saddle bags to check them. He found nothing significant in them.

'OK,' he said. 'Where is the sheriff's watch? And hand over everything else you stole from those dead men.'

'The watch is in my breast pocket.' Benton stood motionless while Hilt relieved him of the watch. Benton's expression had changed to one of desperation, and Hilt watched him closely, ready for anything he might try.

'Let's lock him in the jail,' Errol said impatiently. 'He'll change his mind about not talking when a lynch mob is rattling the door of his cell. He ain't got the sense to see when he is well off.'

'We'll need to get the banker to take

a look at him,' Hilt mused as they escorted Benton along the back lots to the jail.

'I took a bullet out of Leat's shoulder,' Errol said. 'He is at home resting, but he's well enough to point a finger at the men who robbed him.'

'I'll be able to match up the prints of the horse tracks from the rear of the bank all the way out to the ambush spot and then back here to Benton's dun. That should be enough to put a rope around your neck, Benton. A bank teller was killed in the bank raid. So who shot him — Buck Dunne or you? The two of you split up behind that crest after the ambush, and I want to know where Dunne went, and also why you came back to town.'

Benton did not reply. They passed along an alley beside the jail and Errol opened the street door of the law office. Hilt pointed to a chair in front of the desk and Benton sat down. Hilt leaned on the crutch, his right hand close to the butt of his holstered gun.

'I can't waste any more time on this guy, Doc,' said Hilt. 'Buck Dunne left some pretty clear hoof prints back on the ridge when he rode east, and I'd like to get on his trail as soon as possible.'

'I was talking to the town mayor after you went out in my buggy,' Errol said. 'He suggested that you pin on the sheriff's badge temporarily. You're doing the work of a law man right now, so you should be covered legally.'

'I don't think so.' Hilt shook his head. 'I've been after Buck Dunne for months, and I would have got him before he hit the bank here in town if I hadn't been sidetracked. But there's nothing to stop me now. I'll get right after Dunne. I won't stop until I've nailed him, and I don't need to wear a law badge for that chore.'

Hilt became aware that Benton was gazing fixedly at him and wondered at the man's interest.

'Does Dunne know I'm on his trail?' he demanded.

'I don't know anyone named Dunne,' Benton insisted.

'Let's lock him in a cell,' suggested Errol. 'Perhaps a spell behind bars will loosen his tongue.'

Benton was taken into the cell block. Hilt stood by with his pistol in his hand while the doctor acted as a jailer. He was impatient now to take up Dunne's trail and left Errol in the office to return to the saloon. He climbed into the buggy. When he passed the law office on his way back to the ambush spot he saw Doc Errol standing in the doorway. Errol lifted a hand to him and Hilt responded. Relief surged through Hilt's breast as he reached the open range. At last he could renew his hunt for the man who had killed his brother.

4

Buck Dunne was thoughtful as he rode east away from the ambush site. Killing Sheriff Prescott did not cause him one pang of conscience. He had long ago realized that he would prefer to die with his boots on, pursuing the life of crime he had embarked upon in his teens, and twenty years of robbing and killing had hardened him to the ways prevalent in the tough land that was Texas in the nineteenth century. He had taken to the gun readily, and rose quickly to the top of the most wanted list put out by law enforcement officers. He was merciless in his pursuit of easy money, and liked the thrill of killing. He used to keep a strict tally of the number of men he sent to boot hill, but, having reached double figures, no longer bothered.

He was bad tempered and inconsiderate, aggravated by an unnatural impatience, which showed in his heavy features. His pale eyes had the look of a wild beast in their depths, feral and merciless. His normal emotions had evaporated at an early age, leaving him under the influence of the darker side of his nature; plus an undying hatred of law men, and dislike of all other humans. His mother had died of a fever when he was three years old; he had hated his father almost as soon as he could walk, and killed him when he was big enough to take revenge for all the beatings he had suffered at that parent's bullying hands. With no guiding hand to keep him on the straight and narrow trail, he had fallen by the wayside; plunged deeper and deeper into the quagmire of lawlessness; each robbery he committed adding layers of brutality and degradation to his experience.

The knowledge that a number of men inhabited his back trail, all of them sharing the same ambition to kill him, gave him no disquiet. If they pressed too close he merely turned at bay, like a wolf, and his prowess with a pistol always proved to be too good for them. He had learned about Frank Blaine from Ralph Catlin, the former sheriff of Morgan County, recently killed by Blaine, and the fiasco of the bank raid that morning had changed his mind about riding on. Instead, he planned to rob the bank in Cedar Creek again at a later date, and while awaiting the right moment to commit that crime, he would amuse himself by confronting Blaine and killing him.

Not for the first time he checked his surroundings. His hard gaze searched the undulating range, and once, when he thought he spotted movement on his back trail, he turned aside and rode back the way he had come, intent on looking for anyone foolhardy enough to pursue him. He dismounted below a ridge and crawled into a position of observation, remaining motionless for thirty minutes before satisfying himself that he was alone on this part of the range.

His caution was instinctive; an integral part of his make-up. His life depended on his alertness, and he did not begrudge the time it took to ensure that he was not being stalked. That was why he was heading for Diamond O. Sheriff Catlin had mentioned meeting Frank Blaine at the ranch, learned that Blaine's mission in life was to track down and kill Dunne and passed on the information to the outlaw. For his part, Dunne could not remember Thad Hilton, Hilt's brother, but he planned to rid himself of yet another would-be avenger.

When he resumed his original trail, Dunne mused on the vagaries of life along the lawless trail. He'd had a good thing going with Sheriff Catlin, who had been as crooked as a bent nail. Between them they organized a safe area from which to handle their criminal activities. Vince Parker, who owned the Black Ace saloon in Cedar Creek, was another partner in crime, as had been Hank Downey of the Big D, who had joined them because he had rustler blood in his veins. But Blaine and the Texas Rangers had taken out Downey and most of his outfit, and Dunne was planning now to use the Diamond O as a sanctuary.

He stayed off skylines, gradually swung north-west, and was riding through a brush-choked gully when he caught an almost intangible whiff of smoke and burnt cowhide on the breeze. He stopped his horse and stood on the saddle to peer over the rim of the gully. Twenty yards away, three men were bending over a steer that was roped and lying on its side beside a small fire. Dunne's pale eyes glinted when he saw that one of the men was using a running iron on the bawling animal. He showed his yellowed teeth when he recognized one of the trio as a member of Hank Downey's former outfit. He found a break in the wall of the gully, led his horse up out of it, and cantered across the range to where the three men were crouched.

When the sound of his approaching hoofs became apparent, the trio sprang up from the fire and swung around, hands dropping to their holstered pistols. Dunne reined in, grinning.

'Howdy, Foley,' he greeted. 'What in hell are you doing here?'

Cal Foley had half-drawn his Colt, but shoved the weapon back into its holster when he recognized Dunne. Tall and lean, with inscrutable brown eyes, and sharp features mainly covered with black stubble, Foley had a great respect for Dunne's ability with a gun. He grinned and shrugged.

'Heck if it ain't Buck Dunne as large as life,' he replied. 'I thought you were long gone from this neck of the woods. We heard about the bank raid over in Clarkville. The talk is that it was you and your boys did it.'

'So what are you doing blotting brands? That's penny ante stuff.' Dunne slipped his right foot out of his stirrup and hooked his leg around his saddle horn. He reached into his breast pocket for the makings.

'A man has got to make a few dollars how and where he can.' Foley grimaced. 'I guess you heard about Downey and the Big D outfit. We are all that's left of the bunch, and we're down on our bootstraps.'

'There's no need for you boys to ride the chuck line looking for handouts.' Dunne grimaced at the thought. 'As it happens I could do with a few extra guns. How'd you like to hook up with me for a couple of bank jobs? You'd line your pockets in no time.'

'From where I'm standing that sounds like a pretty good idea.' Foley glanced at his two companions. 'This here is Keno Patton,' he introduced, pointing to the nearest of the men, 'and that one is Earl Wallace. What do you reckon, boys? Do we throw in with Buck?'

'We ain't making anything on our own,' Patton observed. 'I ain't had a decent meal since the Rangers put us out of business.'

'I'm all for it,' Wallace grated. 'When can we get to work?'

'Not for a spell,' Dunne replied. 'We had a little trouble at the bank in Cedar Creek this morning, but we'll make up for that later. Right now I'm looking for a place to hole up for a week or so, and I reckon to settle on Diamond O. I heard there's a guy called Blaine working there who has been trailing me because I killed his brother. I reckon to put him out of his misery, and when I've had the chance to work out details of another raid on the bank in Cedar Creek we'll hit them for everything they have and then head for other parts.'

'The Diamond O is the Ormond spread!' Foley grimaced. 'That Sue Ormond is a pretty swell gal. I wouldn't wanta see anything bad happen to her, Buck.'

'Why should it?' Dunne grinned. 'Why don't you three ride into town and nose around? See what you can learn about what happened on Main Street when my boys left the bank. I went out the back door with Hoagy Benton and we missed the action in front. Hoagy is in town now, looking around. You know Hoagy, Foley, so see if he needs any help. Here, take some dough and have yourselves a good time, but don't attract attention to yourselves. Stay in town until I come for you, and tell Hoagy to stay put with you.'

Dunne reached into a pocket and produced a sheaf of greenbacks that had a bank wrapper around it. He removed most of the notes, put them back into his own pocket, and handed the remainder in the wrapper to Foley, who grinned enthusiastically.

'Thanks, boss,' Foley looked at the wrapper and his grin widened. 'Cedar Creek Cattleman's Bank,' he read on it. 'It's fresh from the bank, huh?' He put the dough into a breast pocket. 'We'll be waiting for you in town. Keno, turn that cow loose and let us make tracks out of here. We'll meet up with Hoagy and spend a few dollars — sort of give some of it back to the bank.'

Dunne sat his horse and watched the trio depart. His cunning mind was already turning over possibilities. There were a great number of graves along his back trail, filled with the men he had killed, and he was keen to add one more name to the list: Frank Blaine. He rode on, checking his surroundings, and eventually topped a rise and reined in to study the Diamond O.

The cow spread looked deserted. There were horses in the corral but no men around. It was late afternoon and the sun was brassy in a cloudless, copper-coloured sky. Dunne lifted his Stetson, wiped sweat from his forehead, and checked out each of the buildings ahead. The silence was intense, brooding, throbbing with intensity. He longed for a cool drink, and his pale eyes glinted when he caught a movement at the door of the ranch house as Sue Ormond emerged from the building and dropped wearily into a rocker on the porch.

Dunne touched spurs to his horse and rode openly down the slope toward the yard, acting as if he had every right to be where he was. His gaze did not rest as he approached. He surveyed the bunkhouse, the barn, and looked for riders coming in from outlying pastures. But nothing moved around the spread so he entered the yard and made for the porch.

When Sue Ormond first sighted Dunne she thought he was Frank Blaine returning, and leaned forward in the rocker to identify him, her hopes rising. Disappointment struck her when she realized that it was a stranger approaching, and then fear overcame her, for these days the whole country seemed to be teeming with men intent on causing trouble. She was alone on the ranch except for Billy and her father, Chuck. Billy was in her father's bedroom, trying to soothe the older Ormond. Chuck Ormond was at the difficult stage of his recuperation — not well enough to get up but recovered sufficiently to experience the frustration of having to lie abed when there was work to be done — his constant belly-aching about having to lie in bed had over-stretched Sue's ragged nerves.

Dunne reined in at the porch and looked down at Sue, noting her beauty, and also the alarm showing in her bright eyes. He grinned, keen to reassure her.

'Howdy, miss,' he greeted. 'I heard in town that an old friend of mine, Frank Blaine, was resting up here after a shoot-out, and I've a mind to look him up, seeing that he's hereabouts.'

'I'm afraid you've missed him,' Sue replied. 'He left this morning and won't be coming back. Where did you know Frank?'

'Our trails have crossed a dozen times over the years. We are in the same line of business, you might say. The last I heard of Blaine he was looking for the outlaw Buck Dunne; Dunne hit the bank in Clarkville a while back, so obviously Blaine ain't caught up with

85

him yet.' He glanced around the yard. 'It is mighty quiet around here. Where at is your crew?'

'We've had some trouble. Our outfit was shot to pieces fighting for the brand and we haven't got around to hiring another crew yet.'

'They are still talking about that trouble in Cedar Creek.' Dunne leaned his left hand on his saddle horn. 'Say, I'm at a loose end at the moment. Is there anything I can do to help? My horse is plumb tuckered out, and could sure do with a few days' rest. I can handle any chore on a ranch — was raised on a cow spread in Kansas. I'd work for food only.'

'Thank you, but we're not hiring at the moment.' Sue's tone was resolute.

'OK. Then maybe I could water my horse,' he suggested. 'Then I'll be on my way.'

'Help yourself. If you want food you'll find supplies in the cook shack.' Sue stood up. 'Please forgive me but my father is in bed recovering from a gunshot wound and I must get back to him — he's at the stage of wanting something every moment of the day. You are welcome to feed your horse and yourself before you leave.'

'Thanks, miss.' Dunne turned his horse and rode to the well. He dismounted and hauled a bucket of water for his horse. He drank his fill, using a dipper hanging from the woodwork surrounding the well, before placing the bucket for the horse to drink, and his gaze roamed around the spread. He noted that Sue had re-entered the house, and his eyes narrowed when he saw Billy Ormond appear on the porch and stand watching him. When the horse had slaked its thirst, Dunne led the animal back to the porch.

'Howdy,' he greeted. 'The lady said I could water the horse and then help myself to food from your cook shack.'

'Sure.' Billy nodded. His right hand was down at his side, close to the butt of his holstered gun. 'That's OK. Go ahead and help yourself. Sue said you're an old friend of Frank Blaine.'

'That's right. We've worked together in the past. I'm Joe Colby. I heard Blaine was out here, and I'd like to see him again. Have you any idea where he's headed right now?'

'He rode out this morning. Said he was gonna pick up the trail of Buck Dunne, the outlaw.' Billy was studying Dunne intently as he spoke. There had been a lot of talk in town about Dunne after the bank raid in Clarkville, and a description of the outlaw had been circulated. Billy recalled some of the details he had heard and his suspicions were aroused. This stranger looked very much like Dunne, and his general appearance pointed to the fact that he was not a cowhand; he wore his pistol low down, and the holster was tied to his thigh to facilitate a fast draw. The hair on Dunne's face was red, as was the hair showing under the brim of his Stetson.

Billy kept his expression impassive,

and watched Dunne lead his horse across the yard. He had no intention of bracing the stranger. If it was Dunne then he would be riding on presently. Blaine had left the ranch and was not coming back so there was no danger of him being confronted by the outlaw. Billy sat down in the rocker, and kept an eye on the cook shack after Colby had entered it. Presently, he saw smoke curling up from the chimney, and estimated that the stranger would be gone in about two hours. But his suspicions did not abate, and he was on edge as he waited. He felt vulnerable, being the only able-bodied male on the ranch, and he wished Hilt was still around . . .

*   *   *

Hilt drove the buggy back to the ambush site. He met the buckboard carrying the bodies of Sheriff Prescott and the two posse men returning to town. The liveryman lifted a hand as he passed, but did not stop. Three bodies were lying covered in the buckboard, and three horses were tied behind the vehicle. Hilt continued. He drove down the reverse slope of the crest, checked the hoof prints again, and then set out to trail Buck Dunne. The tracks led to the east, but soon swung north, and Hilt pushed on resolutely. This was the closest he had been to Dunne in many weeks, and eagerness gripped him as he contemplated the impending confrontation.

The hoof prints swung north-west after bypassing Cedar Creek. Hilt frowned when he gazed ahead and realized that he was heading back in the general direction of Diamond O. Cedar Creek was about two miles to his rear when he spotted three riders approaching from ahead. He eased his position on the driving seat of the buggy to make his holstered pistol more accessible. The men spread out slightly as they neared the buggy. Hilt was holding the reins in his left hand. His keen gaze checked the faces confronting him, and he gained a feeling that he had seen one of the men before. He reined in as the trio halted their horses in such a way that impeded further progress of the vehicle.

'Say, you're Frank Blaine, ain't you?' Cal Foley demanded.

'You're right first time,' Hilt replied, 'and I know your face from somewhere, so I reckon you were on the opposite side in the recent shoot-out. As I recall, you were riding with the HD outfit when they attacked Diamond O. We traded lead, and you took off with a hole in your hat.'

Foley's teeth clicked together. He reached for his gun as he called to his two companions.

'Get him! He's trouble.'

Hilt grasped his gun butt as the trio reached for their pistols. He lifted his deadly weapon, and cocked it as he aimed at Foley. The .45 exploded with a crash that threw echoes across the range. Foley jerked at the impact of the

91

slug which smacked into the centre of his chest. His pistol was only half drawn. He lost his grip on the gun as he pitched backwards before twisting and falling lifelessly out of his saddle. Patton and Wallace were surprised by Foley's call for action, and both were slow in grabbing at their gun butts. Patton saw Hilt's gun lining up on him, released his grip on his gun immediately, and threw his hands high and wide in token of surrender even as Hilt's finger trembled in anticipation on his trigger.

Wallace, slightly faster on the draw, cleared leather and lifted his weapon. His teeth were bared in desperation as he thrust his gun hand forward, but, when he saw that Hilt was ahead of him, he triggered a shot before he was fully into the aim and the slug struck the mare, standing motionless between the shafts of the buggy. The animal squealed and went down with threshing hoofs. Hilt was thrown off aim when the buggy jerked as he squeezed his trigger; his bullet smacked into Wallace's right armpit instead of hitting him in the centre of the chest. Wallace lost his gun and swayed in his saddle. Blood spurted from his wound and pain blossomed through him. He fell out of his saddle and grovelled in the bunch grass.

The echoes of the shooting grumbled sullenly into the distance. Gun smoke clawed pungently at Hilt's throat. He breathed shallowly through his open mouth, covering Patton with his pistol as he climbed out of the buggy and leaned his weight on the crutch.

'Get down, and keep your hands in view,' he ordered. 'What's your name, mister?'

'I'm Keno Patton.'

'I thought all the HD crew had been taken care of,' Hilt observed.

Patton dismounted and stood with his hands raised. Hilt looked at the mare, now lying still, and saw blood gushing from the animal's neck. He stomped forward, his weight on the crutch, his pistol in his left hand. He glanced at Foley. The man was lying on his back, his arms outstretched; his discarded gun was just out of reach of his hand. Foley was dying noisily, his rasping breath rattled and wheezed in his throat. His chest, covered in blood, heaved laboriously. His heels drummed against the hard ground and he moaned softly. Hilt watched him until he fell silent and finally relaxed. Patton was gazing in horror at Foley. Wallace was hunched on the ground, his left hand pressed into his right armpit. Blood was seeping through his fingers, and he was fully occupied with his own misfortune. Hilt suspected that his bullet had cut an artery, judging by the amount of blood Wallace was losing.

'You'd better see what you can do for him or he'll bleed to death in a few minutes,' Hilt told Patton. 'If you have any more weapons on you then get rid of them before you move.'

Patton lowered his hands. He dropped to one knee beside Wallace and examined the wound, pressed his fingers against it but failed to stop the bleeding. Panic showed in his expression when he looked up at Hilt.

'I can't stop the bleeding,' he said in a shocked tone. 'What'll I do?'

Hilt peered at the wound and shook his head. 'I reckon he'd die before we'd get him to the doctor in town,' he surmised.

'We can't just stand around and watch him kick over the traces,' rasped Patton. 'Can't you do something to help him?'

'He would have killed me without blinking if I hadn't got him first,' said Hilt, harshly, 'so what do you want me to do — feel sorry for him? Bind the wound and push him back in his saddle if you want to try for the doc, but I think you'll be wasting your time, and I've got other things to do right now.'

He watched Patton remove Wallace's neckerchief and bind it tightly around the wound, but the flow of blood did not decrease. Wallace was ashen-faced.

His eyes were closed. He slumped on the ground and began to shake. In a few moments he was motionless, and Hilt knew he was dead.

Patton got to his feet. His face was grey with shock. He gazed at the blood on his hands, and bent to wipe them on the grass.

'He never had a chance,' said Patton, his lips stiff.

'He would still be alive if he hadn't pulled his gun,' replied Hilt. 'Let's get moving. Unsaddle one of the horses, take the harness off the mare and put it on the horse. We'll go back to Cedar Creek and I'll stick you in the jail. Get moving, and don't make the mistake of trying to get the better of me or you'll wind up dead like your two pards.'

He stood leaning on the crutch while Patton obeyed. The saddle horse did not like the idea of pulling the buggy and became fractious. It lunged forward as soon as the shafts of the buggy were lowered into place. Patton cursed and gripped the reins, using his strength to control the horse. Hilt bent over Wallace and searched the dead man's pockets while keeping an eye on Patton. He found nothing of value and moved to where Foley was lying. He discovered the sheaf of notes in Foley's breast pocket, read the writing on the wrapper, and confronted Patton.

'Where did Foley get this dough from?' Hilt demanded. 'Were you three involved in the bank raid in Cedar Creek this morning?'

'The hell we were!' Patton rasped.

'So how did Foley get his hands on it?'

'We met a man earlier. He gave us the dough.'

'What man?' Hilt pressed. 'Why did he give you the dough?'

'I don't know who he was.' Patton shrugged.

'So a stranger gave you the dough, huh? Do you expect me to believe that? It's more likely you held up and robbed the man. So what really happened? I'm trailing one of the bank robbers. His tracks are plain, and he was heading in this direction. I don't reckon you could have robbed him, so give me the details. And you'd better give it to me straight.'

'I'll do a deal with you,' Patton said, his tone suddenly filled with desperation. 'Turn me loose with that dough and I'll tell you what happened. It was Buck Dunne who we met, and I know where he is heading. You want him for killing your brother, so I heard.'

'Spill it quick,' Hilt rapped. 'If you hold anything back I'll kill you.'

'We saw Dunne at Downey's spread a couple of times. It was him we met this morning. He told us he'd robbed the bank in town but had some trouble, and gave us the money because Foley said we'd join his gang. Dunne is heading for the Diamond O; he said something about holing up there for a few days. That's all I can tell you, Blaine, so give me some of that dough and turn me loose. If you want Dunne you can't waste time taking me back to town so I'll beat it out of here and you won't ever see me again. Is it a deal?'

Hilt shook his head emphatically. 'I can't let you go,' he rapped. 'You're too deeply involved in this business. I'm gonna have to make the time to take you to town so get on your horse and let's go.'

Patton opened his mouth to argue but the expression on Hilt's face prevented him. He turned to his horse and swung into the saddle. Hilt climbed back into the buggy. He held the reins in his left hand, stuck his pistol back into its holster, and picked up the whip. When he cracked the whip over the head of the horse, the animal, being a saddle horse, took exception to being in the shafts and went berserk. It took off in a series of lunging leaps that came close to upsetting the buggy and pitching Hilt headlong out of it.

Patton watched closely as Hilt fought to bring the animal under control; he hoped for a chance of escaping. But Hilt mastered the horse and sent it forward at a canter, Patton kneed his horse into motion and they headed for Cedar Creek. Hilt gritted his teeth as he considered the fact that Dunne was heading for the Diamond O. He realized that Sue could be in the gravest danger while he was forced to ride in the opposite direction and could not go to her aid . . .

5

Hoagy Benton sat disconsolately on a bunk in a cell in the Cedar Creek jail and stared thoughtfully at the bare wall opposite. He was in bad trouble now, and knew it. Damn Buck Dunne! Why hadn't Dunne come into town to discover for himself what had happened to the rest of the gang? No, Dunne was too clever for that! He had sent a saphead to do the dirty work while he rode free and easy — with the money from the bank — and stupid Hoagy Benton was behind bars, carrying the can. Filled with anger at the turn of events, he got restlessly to his feet and went to the door of the cell; gripped the bars and shook the door furiously when it did not budge.

'That won't do you any good,' said a harsh voice from the adjoining cell.

Benton turned and looked at the tall

man lying on the bunk in the next cell. 'Say, I know you!' he exclaimed. 'You're Ben Hussey the gambler who worked in the Black Ace saloon. That guy, Frank Blaine, shot you the other week.'

'Yeah, and he shot a lot of other men after he bested me.' Hussey, tall, slim and dark, put his feet on the floor and stood up. He stretched gingerly, favouring his right shoulder where Hilt's bullet had nailed him. He was wearing a dress shirt which had frills on the front. 'My lawyer is working to get me out of here, and when I'm free I'm gonna see Blaine through gun smoke. You rode with Buck Dunne, I remember. Catlin mentioned you. And my boss, Vince Driver, who owns the Black Ace, has a business interest with Dunne.'

'Yeah, that's right.' Benton nodded. 'I've heard Dunne talking about Parker. They are all in the swim together. But Parker avoided the showdown when Catlin got killed. He's one clever man. That's why I ain't worried too much about being behind bars. We've both got friends who can soon have us out of here.'

'What happened to Dunne's gang this morning?' asked Hussey. 'I heard the shooting when you hit the bank, and they brought two of the bunch in here when it was over. Both had been shot, and died within minutes. The doc told me that five of the gang had been put down. So how did you and Dunne get clear, and what are you doing in here now?'

Benton shook his head. 'Hell if I know!' He spoke in a ragged tone. 'Dunne told me to come in and find out what happened to the rest of the gang. I played it quiet, and was sitting in the diner minding my own business when Frank Blaine came in and got the drop on me.'

'So it was Blaine again, huh?' Hussey laughed mirthlessly. 'I might have known. He sure put a few kinks in the rope Catlin was using around here. And I heard he's been hunting Dunne for months because Buck killed his brother. If Buck ain't careful he'll wind up on boot hill. Blaine is hell on wheels!'

'Dunne is gonna handle Blaine soon as he catches sight of him.' Benton sat down on his bunk. 'So you reckon you'll get out of here?'

'They ain't got a legal charge against me.' Hussey paced the cell with short, impatient steps. 'Catlin would have sprung me before now if Blaine hadn't killed him.' He paused and peered through the bars at Benton. 'What about us busting out of here? If they have got you for robbing the bank then you're facing ten years behind bars. I think the game around here is played out. Anyone with any sense can see that. So I reckon to drift when I do get clear.'

'I'll be lucky if I get ten years,' Benton replied. 'Dunne killed a bank teller this morning, and I reckon they'll pin that on me. I need to get outa here pretty damn quick! If I don't, they'll put a rope around my neck for sure.'

'Will Dunne show up and bust you

out?' Hussey demanded.

'I hope so. He'll hear about me getting caught, and he's always been one for doing what he can for any of the gang, which is now down to just him and me. We need some more guns after the mess we got into this morning. It was sheer bad luck that Blaine happened to be outside the law office when the gang left the bank.'

'Dunne has hit two banks in the county since I've been in here,' said Hussey. 'What's happened to the dough you got from those jobs?

'It's in a safe place. Dunne reckoned to pull out after doing the bank here, and we would have been well in the clear by now if it hadn't all gone wrong.'

'What's to stop Dunne taking all that dough for himself and disappearing across the border? The talk is that's where he's heading.'

Benton shook his head. 'He won't do that,' he said confidently. 'Not while I'm in here. He'll show up and bust me out.'

'But if he doesn't?' Hussey persisted. 'I wouldn't rely on him. Do you know where the money from the robberies is stashed?'

'Sure I do. There's no secret about that. The dough doesn't belong to Dunne just because he bosses the gang.'

'So why don't we bust out of here, grab that dough for ourselves, and hit Mexico together?' Hussey suggested.

'Are you kidding?' Benton laughed cynically. 'I wouldn't do that to Buck Dunne for all the money in the world. He'd come after me for sure, and he'd go through Hell to get me in his sights. I don't want that kind of trouble on my tail.'

'Think about it.' Hussey sat down and relaxed. 'You've got plenty of time, and when Dunne doesn't show up to bust you out you just might change your mind about looking out for yourself. If you stick around you're gonna get a rope around your neck, huh?'

Benton rubbed his chin reflectively,

his eyes narrowed. He didn't like the thoughts that Hussey's words had conjured up in his mind. But he knew Dunne, and was certain the outlaw boss would free him from the law. He stretched out on the bunk and tried to relax, but his restlessness was such that he got to his feet again and began to pace the cell relentlessly. Dunne had better show up, he thought angrily. If he didn't then there would be hell to pay!

* * *

Buck Dunne sat in the cook shack at Diamond O and ate the meal he had cooked. Twice he got up from his seat and peered out of the window to check the approaches to the ranch. The heat of the sun had turned the shack into an oven and he sweated freely. He longed for the cool of the evening, and could not wait for the time when he would cross into Mexico, find a quiet place to lie low, and begin to live like a man instead of a hunted animal.

He heard a noise outside the shack and drew his Colt. His eyes glittered and his alertness was at full pitch as he went to the window again. He saw nothing suspicious around the yard, but sensed that someone was outside the shack. It was probably the youngster who lived at the ranch, he thought. Dunne had seen suspicion in Billy's eyes back there at the house.

Dunne opened the door of the shack and peered out. He stepped outside and skirted the building silently, his gun ready, and when he passed around a rear corner he saw Billy Ormond standing at the front corner, holding a pistol in his right hand.

'What do you reckon to do with that gun?' Dunne demanded.

Billy jumped as if he had been shot. He did not turn around, and lowered his right hand to his side, the pistol pointing at the ground.

'I'm just checking out the spread,' Billy said tensely. 'We've had a lot of trouble around here lately, and some of the badmen are still lurking on the range. I have to be careful because my pa is in bed with a bad wound and we don't have an outfit any more.'

'You don't have to worry about anyone while I'm around,' Dunne said. 'Drop your gun because you're making me feel nervous. I reckon to stick around here for a few days and I don't want you to get any ideas about moving me on. If you do like you're told then there won't be any trouble, and you'll still be breathing when I do leave.'

'There's nothing around here for you,' Billy protested, opening his hand and letting his gun fall to the ground. He raised his hands shoulder high.

'Put them down,' Dunne rapped. 'We'll go over to the house and remove any guns you might have around. If we keep temptation out of your way then there won't be any trouble.'

'You're Buck Dunne, the outlaw, huh?' Billy demanded.

'You got it. So now you know where you stand,' Dunne grinned. 'I'm gonna hide out here for a spell so don't even think about giving me any hassle. Let's go tell your sister what is going on. I don't want trouble so don't start any unless you wanta die quick. Now get moving.'

Dunne bent and scooped up Billy's pistol as the youngster led the way across the yard to the house. Billy was angry with himself for thinking that he could take the notorious Buck Dunne with no trouble. Now he had given the game away and Dunne had the upper hand, Billy suffered no illusions about his fate if he did not do as he was told. Dunne holstered his pistol when they reached the porch and Billy led the way into the house. Dishes were rattling in the kitchen, and Billy called his sister. Sue came to the kitchen door, wiping her hands on a cloth; her expression changed when she saw Dunne standing behind Billy.

'What's going on?' she demanded.

'I've decided to stick around here for a few days,' Dunne replied. 'I won't trouble anyone here if I'm not bothered by you. Is that a deal?'

Sue frowned. She noticed that Billy's holster was empty.

'You better do like he says, Sue,' Billy said softly. 'He's Buck Dunne, the outlaw, and he means business.'

'No one need get hurt,' Dunne said. 'I want every gun you've got in the house. You get on with what you're doing in the kitchen, Miss. Your brother will show me around looking for spare weapons. Don't make any mistake about this. I'll shoot to kill at the first sign of resistance. Just do like I tell you and no one will get hurt.'

Sue nodded and returned to the kitchen. Dunne pushed Billy and set him into motion.

'Spare guns,' he said. 'There'll be some around, I guess.'

Billy went into the big living room, where a Winchester .44–.40 was hanging above the fireplace. Dunne took down the weapon and checked it; he found it fully loaded. He tucked the

111

butt under his right armpit. Billy opened a cupboard and produced his father's gun belt and pistol. Dunne took the belt and swung it over his left shoulder.

'Keep looking,' he ordered. 'There's no telling what you'll find. Just bear in mind that if I do find any weapons after we've searched the house then I'll shoot you between the eyes.'

'You've got all the guns there are.' Billy was shaking inside, but not from fear. He was furious with himself for capitulating so tamely, and he would take any opportunity to get the better of Dunne.

'Let's take a look upstairs,' Dunne said. 'Remember what I told you — I'll start shooting if you give me cause to worry.

'There are no weapons up there,' Billy replied. 'My father is in bed. He was badly wounded, and shouldn't be disturbed.'

'Taking a look at him won't hurt anybody,' Dunne grinned. 'But the situation could change drastically if you get frisky.'

Billy did not reply. He led the way up the stairs, recalling all that he had heard about Dunne. It was said that the outlaw never passed up an opportunity to shoot someone. He was an out-and-out killer!

Dunne satisfied himself that there were no more weapons in the house. 'OK,' he said, taking the rifle in his left hand. 'You're doing OK so keep it up. I want you to stay in the kitchen with your sister. Don't go roaming around the house because it'll make me nervous. Just stay put and don't get any ideas about besting me because it ain't likely to happen.'

They descended the stairs, and Dunne called a halt as they reached the bottom step. His gun appeared in his hand so fast that Billy did not see the movement.

'I can hear a rider coming,' Dunne said. 'Take a look out the window and see who it is. Don't show yourself.'

Billy went to a front window and peered out across the yard. He saw a rider approaching, and a flicker of hope speared through him when he recognized John Fletcher, the new deputy in Cedar Creek.

'Who is it?' Dunne demanded.

Billy told him and Dunne cocked his pistol.

'Don't shoot him,' Billy said sharply. 'He's coming to see my sister. He's sweet on her. He won't give you any trouble if you get the drop on him.'

'Get rid of him,' Dunne retorted, 'and don't try to warn him about me.'

Billy stepped into the open doorway and waited until Fletcher reined in at the porch.

'Howdy, Fletch,' he greeted. 'What are you doing this far out of town? Say, you ain't wearing your deputy badge.'

'Hi, Billy!' Fletcher responded. 'I ain't wearing the badge because I quit. I reckon to come and ride for you, knowing you're short-handed. I'm not cut out to be a law man. The Dunne

114

gang hit the bank in Cedar Creek this morning and there was hell to pay. Five of Dunne's gang were shot down in the street; the bank clerk was killed, and Mr Leat, the banker, was shot real bad. And as if that wasn't bad enough, Ike Prescott and three posse men pursued Dunne and another outlaw. They walked into an ambush south of town and Ike and two posse men were killed. Heck, I like a quiet life so I quit on the spot.'

'Sue ain't here at the moment, Fletch,' Billy interrupted. 'She rode over to the Taggart place first thing this morning. Mrs Taggart has got a fever so Sue went to help. I'm sorry you've had your long ride for nothing, but Sue is bossing things here while Pa is laid up, and she refuses to take on another crew. I've tried to talk her round to my way of thinking, but nothing is being done around here right now.'

'Heck, I was counting on getting a job here,' Fletcher said. 'You know I can turn my hand to anything on a ranch. Give me a few days' work to earn some eating money, huh? Surely you can manage that.'

'I said get rid of him,' Dunne hissed in Billy's ear.

'Sorry, Fletch, I can't do that. Sue has said no and I can't go against her word.'

'I thought we were friends, Billy,' Fletcher said.

Dunne uttered an imprecation and stepped forward to get a view of Fletcher. He raised his pistol. Billy realized that for a moment he was not covered by Dunne's Colt and reached out to grasp the outlaw's gun arm. He forced the limb upwards and tried to pull the pistol out of Dunne's hand. Dunne swung his left fist and crashed his knuckles against Billy's jaw. Billy's knees buckled, but he clung on desperately, and butted his head forward to smash his forehead into Dunne's face.

Fletcher reacted quickly when he caught a glimpse of Dunne. He jumped off his horse and ran on to the porch, intending to go to Billy's aid. Dunne was reeling back from Billy with blood streaming from his damaged nose. He pushed Billy through the open door to the porch and Billy collided with the fast-moving Fletcher. Dunne lifted his pistol and fired a shot into Fletcher's chest. The ex-deputy staggered and then dropped to the porch. Billy fell against the door jamb after bouncing off Fletcher. He hit the floor but sprang up quickly. He heard Dunne's shot, saw Fletcher fall away, and hurled himself desperately at Dunne.

Dunne jerked his pistol in Billy's direction. Billy reached out to grapple with the outlaw. Dunne thrust his gun muzzle into Billy's stomach and squeezed the trigger. Billy cried out and fell on his face. Dunne stepped back and looked around. He heard Sue calling out as she emerged from the kitchen. He turned to face her as she came running through the doorway.

'I told him no trouble,' Dunne rasped. 'How stupid can you get, huh?'

Sue dropped to her knees beside Billy. She saw blood staining his stomach and pressed her hand against his chest. There was no heartbeat. She turned her head and looked up at Dunne with shock-filled eyes.

'He's dead!' she cried. 'You've killed him.'

Dunne stepped around her and bent over the motionless Fletcher. 'And he's dead,' he announced. 'They got what they asked for, trying to get the better of me.'

Sue slumped over Billy's body, sobbing bitterly. Dunne watched her for a moment before shaking her shoulder.

'Get back into the kitchen,' he rasped. 'I warned him not to try anything. You better mind your manners after this.'

Sue ignored Dunne and he grasped her arm and hauled her to her feet.

'Quit the wailing,' he snarled. 'It ain't doing any good. He'd still be alive if he'd done like I said.'

Sue staggered away, left hand outstretched as if she were walking in her sleep. She entered the kitchen and slammed the door. Dunne stood for a moment, looking down at the two bodies. He took hold of Billy by the scruff of the neck, dragged him out of the doorway and dumped him off the end of the porch, and then did the same with John Fletcher. He remained on the porch, gazing out across the range, his mind flitting over the situation, aware that the shooting had changed everything: it would no longer be sensible to stay on at the ranch.

He turned abruptly, walked across the yard to the corral, and saddled his horse. He entered the cook shack for supplies, and then swung into his saddle and rode away without looking back. When he was out of sight of the house be began to circle towards Cedar Creek. He had to take a chance on going into town because he needed to contact Benton. They would cut their losses and pull out, but fast.

Hilt sighed with relief when he sighted Cedar Creek. Patton had given him no trouble on the ride to town. They traversed the street and halted in front of the law office; Hilt climbed out of the buggy, his gun in his left hand. He leaned heavily on the crutch, watching Patton intently as the man dismounted. Patton, his face sullen, opened the door of the office and entered with Hilt at his back. Pete Maxwell was seated at the desk in the office. He sprang up when he recognized Hilt.

'Who have you got here?' Maxwell demanded. 'It ain't Buck Dunne, that's for sure.'

'Are you the new sheriff?' Hilt demanded.

'No, I'm standing in until they can get a new man.'

'This is Keno Patton,' Hilt said. 'He rode for Big D until we put them out of business. I'm in a hurry to get back on Dunne's trail. Stick Patton behind bars and hold him until I get back. I need to go out to Diamond O. I believe Dunne is headed there, and there could be bad trouble at the ranch right now.'

Maxwell drew his gun. Hilt remained long enough to see Patton locked in a cell before departing. Then he climbed into the buggy and set out fast for Diamond O. Time seemed to stand still as he cracked the whip and pushed the horse along at its best pace. The buggy rolled and bumped over the undulating trail. Hilt's leg wound protested painfully at the rough treatment it was receiving, but he pushed on, driving the horse hard; nagged by the fear that Sue Ormond might be in bad trouble and aware that he was the only one who could help her.

It was late afternoon when he finally saw the roof of the Diamond O ranch house in the distance. He stopped the buggy in cover and left the sweating horse with trailing reins. He drew his pistol, checked the weapon, and then stomped through the brush towards the spread. He cursed his wounded leg as he made heavy work of the short trip. Sweat was beading his forehead and dripping down his face by the time he reached the yard.

Hilt stayed under cover and studied the ranch. Nothing moved; a heavy silence hung over the clustered buildings. He looked over at the corral, where several horses were penned, all standing motionless in the heat of the afternoon, their tails swishing incessantly. Hilt wondered if Dunne was around. He stirred himself, knowing there was only one way to find out. He took a fresh grip on his pistol and moved to his right until he was facing a side of the house where there were no windows. He slipped through a gap in the fence and made his way to the shelter of the nearest wall before moving silently to the rear of the building to peer around the corner and check out the back yard.

The kitchen door was closed; Hilt approached it. He peered cautiously through a window, saw the kitchen was deserted, and tried the door only to find it was locked. He went on around the house and down the opposite side towards the porch. When he saw two bodies lying by the side of the porch he halted abruptly. Shock hit him hard when he bent over them and recognized Billy Ormond: dead with a stomach wound. He checked the other body and recognized Fletcher as the deputy he had spoken to in town.

So Dunne was here, Hilt thought. This was a prime example of his handiwork. He cocked his gun and stepped on to the porch, leaning heavily on the crutch, his thoughts fixed on Sue. He peered through a window into the big front room, saw it was deserted, and almost lost his balance when he moved to the front door. He propped the crutch against the wall and went into the house without it, endeavouring to keep most of his weight off the wounded limb.

The house was as silent as boot hill on a wet Sunday afternoon. Hilt listened intently for unnatural sound. He heard nothing, and when he was satisfied that he was alone he began a search of the ground floor rooms. He found nothing, and his thoughts turned to Chuck Ormond — the wounded rancher would be up in his bedroom. Hilt ascended the stairs, his pistol cocked and ready. He felt frozen inside; numbed by the shock of discovering Billy Ormond lying dead, aware that he might have prevented this tragedy if he had not been delayed on the trail by Foley and Patton.

He searched the other bedrooms, which were empty, before turning his attention to Chuck Ormond's bedroom. He stood before the closed door for some moments, an ear to a panel, listening intently, but heard nothing. He drew a deep breath and restrained it for a moment before grasping the door handle and turning it slowly. Then he thrust the door open and lunged into the room, his pistol flicking around as he looked for a target.

Chuck Ormond was lying in bed, his eyes closed. Sue was kneeling beside the bed with her face in her hands. She was silent and still, her shoulders shaking convulsively. Buck Dunne was not present.

'Sue,' Hilt called softly. He raised his voice and called her name again.

Sue started, raised her head, and turned her tear-stained face towards the door. She began to cry when she saw Hilt, and he went to her side and lifted her gently to her feet.

'What happened here?' he asked in a harsh whisper.

She told him in a wavering tone, and Hilt clenched his teeth as he listened. If only he had not been so impatient, he thought. It was his fault this had happened because he should have been on the ranch when Dunne showed up.

'Is Dunne still around?' he asked.

Sue shook her head. 'I saw him ride out,' she replied. 'He rode north, and when he crossed a ridge I went out to check on him. As soon as he was out of sight of the spread he circled and headed towards Cedar Creek.'

Hilt stifled a groan. 'Jeez, I've just come from there! I'd better head back as fast as I can. Dunne has probably gone to find a man he left behind in town when he rode on here. I don't like leaving you, Sue, but you shouldn't have any more trouble now. If I can catch up with Dunne I'll put him where he belongs.'

'You must do what you have to,' she replied tonelessly. 'I have to stay here with my father.'

'I'll come back as soon as I can,' he responded.

He took his leave although he wished he could stay. He picked up his crutch and stomped resolutely across the yard, heading back to where he had left the buggy. His leg was aching intolerably by the time he climbed into the vehicle. The horse cavorted, and almost turned the buggy over, but eventually settled down and hammered along the trail at a gallop.

Hilt rode through the approaching evening. Shadows were closing in on the trail by the time he saw lights gleaming in Cedar Creek; stars glistened remotely in the darkening sky and a cooling breeze was blowing from the west. By the time Hilt hauled on the reins in front of the law office he was impatient to get out of the torturous buggy, and almost fell out of the vehicle in his haste to stand erect. He leaned on the crutch and lifted his aching right leg to take his weight off it.

The town seemed quiet. He paused to look around. He needed a drink and a meal, but his comfort would have to wait. He staggered on to the sidewalk and approached the door of the law office. When he tried the door he discovered that it was locked, although there was a light burning inside the office. He peered through the front window and saw the office was empty. He wondered if Buck Dunne was in town, skulking around to find out what had happened to Hoagy Benton. He suppressed a sigh as he stomped along the sidewalk towards the diner. Pete

Maxwell was probably at supper right now.

The diner was crowded. Hilt stood in the doorway looking around at the faces turned towards him. He could not see Maxwell, but John Ketchum, the liveryman, was seated at a nearby table eating his supper. Hilt joined Ketchum, who stopped eating to look at him.

'What's been going on around here?' Hilt asked. 'Have you seen Pete Maxwell? He ain't in the law office.'

'Pete is dead,' Ketchum replied dourly. 'He was shot down on the street about two hours ago. No one saw it happen.'

Hilt shook his head at the news. Buck Dunne had to be responsible, he thought. Perhaps the outlaw had learned that Benton was in jail and was preparing to free him.

'Have you seen any strangers around?' he asked.

Ketchum shook his head and resumed eating.

'Is anyone guarding the prisoners?' Hilt persisted.

'No one will take on the job now Pete is dead,' Ketchum said through a mouthful of food. 'Nobody wants to get shot. There's been a lot of killing around here today, and everyone is scared of being the next victim. Doc Errol has been trying to get a couple of men to sit in the law office and guard the prisoners, but no one wants to know.'

'I'd better see the doc.' Hilt got to his feet and left the diner.

Darkness had fallen and he looked around, wondering where Dunne was at that moment. He walked back along the sidewalk, and spotted a figure at the door of the law office. He dropped a hand to the butt of his gun and hurried along, hoping to accost Dunne.

'Hold on there,' Hilt called, as the figure turned away from the office.

The man paused and turned to confront Hilt. Lamp light fell upon his face. Hilt relaxed. It was Doc Errol, holding a bunch of keys. Errol shrugged. His face was lined with worry.

'I just heard about Pete Maxwell getting killed, Doc,' Hilt said. 'Have you got anyone to guard your prisoners?'

'No luck,' Errol replied. 'How did you get on? Did you catch up with Dunne?'

Hilt explained the situation he had found at the ranch.

Errol shook his head. 'I'd better go out there and do what I can for Sue. She'll be devastated by Billy's death. That killer has got to be stopped, Blaine.'

'Just let me see him,' Hilt said grimly. 'I'm having nothing but bad luck at the moment, but it will change for the better. Give me those keys, Doc. Dunne headed back in this direction when he left Diamond O and I have a feeling he'll try to bust Benton out of jail. If that is the case then I want to be on hand to confront him. Is that OK by you?'

'I'd like nothing better,' Errol said eagerly. He unlocked the door of the office. 'I've just checked on the prisoners and they've settled down for the night. I can't stand guard because I'm expecting a call that will take me out of town for several hours. I'll see you some time in the morning. I'll take the buggy in case I need it tonight.'

Hilt took the bunch of keys and limped into the office. Errol departed quickly, as if afraid that Hilt would change his mind. Hilt closed and locked the street door and then sat down at the desk towards the rear of the office. He was as ready as he would ever be to confront Buck Dunne, and hoped the outlaw would show up.

6

Buck Dunne timed his return to Cedar Creek to coincide with the onset of night. He spotted the lights of the town from far off, but remained on the outskirts until full darkness had fallen. When his movements were cloaked by shadows he rode across the back lots to the rear of the Black Ace saloon and tethered his mount behind the store house there. He entered the saloon by the back door and made his way to Vince Parker's office. He and Parker were friends of long-standing. Both were highly satisfied with their business arrangements, but, when Dunne walked in on the saloon proprietor, Parker sprang up from his desk in shock.

'What in hell are you doing here, Buck?' Parker, tall, powerful, and rugged, was wearing a light blue suit and a string tie. He was a handsome man who took pains with his appearance. His face was clean-shaven; the hair on his head, black as a raven's wing, was neatly trimmed and well greased with sweet-smelling oil redolent of prairie flowers. He sat down in his seat and gazed at Dunne with surprise in his brown eyes.

'It has been one of those days, Vince,' Dunne replied. 'I should have stayed in my blankets today, and would have done if I'd known what was going to happen. But I'm only gonna be here long enough to collect Hoagy Benton and then we'll be long gone to Mexico.'

'Benton is in jail.' Parker produced a cigar case from an inside pocket of his jacket, selected a cigar, and went through the motions of lighting it, his hard gaze never leaving Dunne's fleshy face. His low tone was loaded with irritation. 'So what happened at the bank? How come you got caught with your guard down? Five of your bunch died in the shoot-out. Then the sheriff and two of his posse men were gunned down in an ambush. Later, I heard, Benton walked around town like he owned the place and was jailed for his nerve. Then Pete Maxwell, who was standing in for the law until they can get another sheriff, was shot down in cold blood on the street a couple of hours ago.'

'Who shot him?' Dunne demanded.

'I thought it was you!'

'Hey, it wasn't me! I didn't get back here until it was dark, so I plead not guilty. It must have been one of your men. Ben Hussey is still in jail, huh? So someone decided it was time to spring him, I guess. If Hoagy is in jail then I'll walk in there and bust him loose.'

'You'd better stay clear of more trouble,' Parker observed. 'As I hear it, no one in town wants the job of jailer or sheriff, so there won't be a guard in the law office tonight. I was thinking of sending a couple of my men along there to open it up. There won't be a better time than tonight so I'll arrange it. When Benton is in the clear you'd better ride out and stay away until the heat cools, huh?'

'Sure. I'll head into Mexico as soon as I can. I have some unfinished business to handle around here but that will have to wait. I'll lie low for a couple of months before I come back and clean out the bank in this burg. I still don't know what went wrong today, but I'll recruit a new gang and we'll finish the job some other time.'

'That's the way,' Parker agreed. 'No sense stirring up a hornets' nest. Doc Errol is trying to rouse the town to action, so give them time to cool down. Why don't you rest up here until I get the jail break organized? If you go wandering around town you'll sure as hell be recognized, and we don't need any more trouble on top of what we've already got.'

'Gimme a bottle of redeye and I'll go along with that suggestion.' Dunne grinned. 'I left my horse behind your store house out back. Get someone to put it under cover. I want to ride out before sunup, so have Benton out of jail by then.'

Parker got to his feet. 'Just sit tight until I get back,' he said. 'There's a bottle of my best whiskey in the bottom right drawer of the desk. I'll get Farris and Clinton moving. They'll bust the jail with no trouble at all.'

Dunne took over Parker's seat behind the desk when the saloon man departed, and reached for the bottle of whiskey in the bottom drawer. Parker went into the saloon and paused to look over the crowded room. A knot of townsmen stood at the bar talking about the events of the day; an undercurrent of excitement was throbbing in the room like a festering sore. Parker ascended the flight of stairs that led up to his private quarters and paused at the top beside a big man seated on a chair with a Winchester across his knees who was watching the bar room intently.

'Farris, I've got a job for you,' Parker said.

Bull Farris stood up immediately. He stood head and shoulders over Parker, who was completely dwarfed by his huge employee.

'Anything you say, Boss,' Farris replied. He was massively built, with broad shoulders and large hands. His face was shapeless — a great blob of flesh with a large, misshapen nose in its centre and a trap-like mouth beneath. There was much scar tissue around both his deep set brown eyes. His voice was hoarse and low-pitched. He was wearing a store suit which was half a size too small; the jacket was over-stretched across his chest and the shoulders were strained out of shape by his bulk. He was a formidable figure; normally easy-tempered and non-aggressive until he was aroused, when it usually took six men to restrain him when he did cut loose.

'Get Clinton out from behind the bar and bring him to my office,' Parker said. 'It's time we got Ben Hussey out of the jail.'

'Sure, Boss.' Farris started down the stairs immediately. Parker waited a few moments before returning to his office, where Dunne had moved to a leather couch against the back wall and was lounging on it, a whiskey bottle in his hand.

'I always said you had the right idea, Vince,' Dunne observed. 'You've got this set-up and nothing to do all day, and I'm in the saddle night and day trying to make ends meet. I'll swap with you if you've a mind to change your life around. I'm getting a mite tired these days of dodging the law.'

'No dice,' Parker replied. 'Have you forgotten that we robbed a couple of banks when we first started out? I put my loot into this business while you wasted yours and had to keep robbing to live. I told you long ago to get out of that game, and you would be sitting pretty right now if you'd taken my advice.'

'I need excitement,' Dunne replied. 'I've done all right in my way — I've got plenty of dough stashed away. Maybe I will splash out and buy a business at that.' His pale eyes glinted as he considered. 'How's this for an idea? I was at the Diamond O earlier and had to kill Billy Ormond. There is only the old man, Chuck Ormond, and a gal out there, and if something happened to them the place will come up for sale.'

'Are you fixing to murder them in cold blood?' Parker demanded. 'Hell, you couldn't get away with that!'

'You could buy the spread when it comes up for sale and I'll give you the dough for it. I don't have to kill those folks. I could hold them out there until the old man signs the place over to me, and that way I'd get it for nothing.'

'I don't like the sound of that,' Parker said sharply. 'I've just bought Hank Downey's Big D ranch and plan to live there when I get out of this business. I've always fancied running a few cows. But you forget about Diamond O, Buck. I wouldn't want you as a near neighbour. You'd attract too much attention. Your best bet is to head into Mexico

139

and stay there until the heat is off.'

'So the smart money around here is going into the cattle business, huh? You're playing a close game, Vince. OK, I'll let Diamond O go for now, but I won't forget it.'

'The difference between you and me, Buck, is that I've got a good reputation and you're running crooked.'

There was a knock at the door of the office. Dunne dropped the bottle of whiskey and drew his pistol.

'Relax,' Parker told him. 'That'll be Farris and Clinton.'

Dunne holstered his gun and picked up the whiskey bottle. Some of the spirit had spilled on the floor. He took a long swig from the bottle as Parker opened the office door. Farris and Clinton entered. Farris blocked the doorway completely, and paused when he recognized Dunne. Clinton, a medium-sized man with narrow, sloping shoulders and a skinny body, pushed Farris in the back and the big man moved quickly to one side. Parker closed the door, went behind his desk, and sat down in his leather upholstered seat.

'It is time we busted Hussey out of jail,' said Parker. 'And Hoagy Benton, who is also behind bars. You know Benton, Farris?'

'Sure, Boss. I've seen him around. Do you want Clinton and me to do the job?'

'That's the general idea. Let Clinton work out the details and go along with what he says. There shouldn't be a jailer in the office so you won't have any trouble. Get Hussey and Benton out and bring them back here. We'll be waiting for you. Have you got that?'

'No sweat,' Clinton said. 'We'll mosey along there now and do the job.'

'You'll need to get into the office and find the cell keys,' Parker said. 'You won't open the cells unless you do. No shooting, and don't make any noise. I don't want you getting traced back to this saloon.'

'Sure, Boss.' Farris grinned. He pushed Clinton towards the door.

'Make a move, pard. I wanta be back in time for supper.'

They left the saloon and Clinton led Farris along the sidewalk towards the jail. 'You heard what the boss said, Farris — no noise! You'd better keep watch while I do the job.'

'The boss said there wouldn't be a jailer inside.' Farris paused at the door of the law office. 'Say, there's a lamp burning inside. Someone must be in there.'

Clinton approached the front window and peered through the dusty glass. Farris pushed him out of his way and bent to look into the office.

'There's no one inside,' he observed. 'So why is the lamp alight?'

'Maybe they want folks to think there is someone inside,' Clinton suggested. 'How are we gonna get in without making a noise? The place is built like a fort.'

Farris tried the door, and shook it when he found it locked.

'Cut it out,' Clinton warned. 'You're

142

making too much noise.'

Farris glanced around the darkened street. 'There's no one around,' he declared. He leaned against the door, felt it give a fraction, and then eased back and slammed his shoulder against it. The lock gave way and the door flew inwards. Farris blundered over the doorstep and finished up on his hands and knees on the threshold of the office. Clinton looked around the street but the sound of the door breaking seemed to have passed unnoticed. He entered the office and closed the door.

'You stand just inside the door and keep an eye on the street in case anyone shows up,' Clinton said. He went to check the connecting door in the back wall of the office, found it locked, and went to the desk. A brief search failed to produce the cell keys and he motioned to the watchful Farris. 'See if you can open the door to the cells without making too much noise,' he said.

Farris crossed the office and tried the inner door. He stepped back a pace, raised his right foot, and smashed his boot against the door in the region of the lock. The door splintered and part of the lock fell to the floor. Farris grinned at Clinton and waved a hand for the smaller man to precede him into the cell block.

Clinton went through the doorway; a lantern illuminated the cells. Clinton halted when he noted that the door of one of the cells was half-open. He saw a man holding a pistol getting up from the bunk in the cell and, too surprised to react, watched him come forward.

Hilt, disturbed from sleep, emerged from the cell with his pistol levelled. 'Who are you?' he demanded. 'What's the idea busting in here like that?'

Clinton raised his hands instantly. Behind him, Farris peered around the doorpost, and ducked back when he saw Hilt and the levelled gun. Hilt side-swiped Clinton with the barrel of the pistol, and then stepped over the man's falling body to menace Farris, who had drawn his pistol and turned to fight. He fired the instant Hilt appeared in the doorway and his bullet splintered the door jamb beside Hilt's left ear. Gun smoke flared and the racket of the shot reverberated through the jail. Hilt squeezed off a shot as his foresight lined up on the big man. The slug hit Farris in the chest and he fell to his knees as if his legs had been cut off with an axe. He tried to bring his pistol to bear on Hilt but his immense strength deserted him and he dropped the weapon.

Hilt cocked his gun for a second shot but held his fire when Farris fell forward on to his face. He limped forward and picked up Farris's discarded gun before turning his attention to Clinton, who was struggling to regain his feet and beginning to draw his gun.

'Forget about the gun,' Hilt snapped. 'Drop it.'

Clinton froze, looked into the muzzle of Hilt's pistol, and then released his hold on the Colt. The weapon fell to the floor. Clinton raised his hands.

'Who are you?' Clinton demanded. 'I was told there was no one in here tonight.'

'So who are you?' Hilt countered. He motioned to the cell in which he had been sleeping. 'Get in there. There's a bunch of keys on the bunk. Pass them out to me and make yourself comfortable. If you're so keen to come in, then you can stay.'

Clinton gazed at Hilt's gun and shrugged. He entered the cell, located the bunch of keys, and tossed it out to Hilt, who locked the cell door on him.

'So you and your pard came in to bust out the prisoners, huh?' Hilt demanded. 'Who told you the place would be unguarded?'

'They said no one wanted the job of jailer,' Clinton explained.

'Tell me who you are and what you do around town,' Hilt persisted.

'I'm a bartender at the Black Ace. My name is Clinton.'

Hilt nodded. 'So you were after Hussey, huh? OK, now take a look at the prisoner in the other cell. Do you know who he is?'

Clinton looked in the direction Hilt was pointing and saw Hoagy Benton sitting up on his bunk in the cell beyond Hussey.

'No,' he lied. 'I never saw him before. Who is he?'

Hilt did not reply. He went into the office and bent over the motionless Farris. The big man was alive but unconscious. A noise at the street door alerted Hilt and he swung around to see Doc Errol pushing open the door. Errol was holding a Colt in his right hand and his medical bag in his left.

'I heard a shot,' Errol said, 'and I reckoned it came from here. He went to Farris and dropped to one knee. 'What happened?'

Hilt explained, and then asked. 'Do you know who he is, Doc?'

Errol nodded. 'He is Bull Farris, a guard at the Black Ace saloon; a

147

strong-arm man for Vince Parker, who owns the saloon.'

'There's a guy named Clinton in one of the cells. He came in with Farris. They were planning to spring Hussey. What's Parker like? Could he be in on this? I don't see these two acting on their own. Hussey has been in jail over a month. Why spring him now?'

Errol shrugged. 'On the face of it Parker runs a straight business, but he's got some men working for him who are doubtful.'

'Have you got anyone who will take over here in the morning?' Hilt asked. 'I shouldn't have left Sue Ormond out at Diamond O like I did, but I can't afford to lose Buck Dunne now. He headed back in this direction after leaving Diamond O, and I'm wondering where he could be holed up right now. I ought to ride out to the Ormond ranch first thing, pick up Dunne's tracks, and trail him to where he's gone to ground. Dunne didn't know Benton is behind bars, and when he does learn about it I reckon he'll come in here to bust him loose. So that's my problem. Do I sit here and wait in the hope that Dunne will show up, or do I get on his trail again and try to run him down?'

'No one I've spoken to about taking over here is keen on the job,' Errol said. 'I'm not surprised, the way Sheriff Prescott was gunned down. You're the only man I know who has the necessary skill and nerve to handle the job, Hilt. Won't you consider stepping into Prescott's boots? You've more than proved yourself against badmen, and with a law badge on your chest you would have a lot more power when you go after Dunne.'

'I wasted a lot of time when I took up with the Ormonds.' Hilt shook his head. 'I'd have nailed Dunne long before now if I'd minded my own business and stuck to his trail. Do you think you could get a man to go out to Diamond O tomorrow and help Sue Ormond? Billy is lying dead beside the porch, and the young man who was wearing a deputy badge when I saw him around here earlier is with him. Dunne shot them both.'

'John Fletcher. So that's where he went! I heard he was sweet on Sue.' Errol shook his head. 'I can promise you that someone will go out to help the Ormonds if you'll take over the law around here. What have you got to lose? You can quit as soon as you get Dunne.'

Hilt nodded. 'OK. It's a deal,' he said. 'I need to wrap up my fight with Dunne. He's spilling blood where ever he goes, and there is only one thing that will stop him.'

'I'll go tell Mayor Hartford of your decision. Then I'll have Farris taken along to my place. I'll also get hold of a carpenter to come and fix this door.' Errol hurried out of the office as if afraid that Hilt would change his mind.

Hilt called after him: 'See if you can find a couple of men to act as deputies. If you can, I'll be able to concentrate on getting Dunne.'

Errol lifted a hand in acknowledgement and hurried off along the street.

Hilt went to the street door and inspected the damage. The lock was broken so he fetched a high-backed chair and jammed it under the inside handle. He went to the desk and sat down, impatient now for morning to arrive . . .

★ ★ ★

In the saloon, Parker started up from his desk when he heard shooting. Dunne was sprawled on the couch, drinking occasionally from the whiskey bottle he was clutching in his left hand.

'Did you hear that?' Parker demanded.

'Hear what?' Dunne took another swig from the bottle, discovered it was empty and tossed it into a corner of the office. 'Give me another bottle, Vince.'

'I heard shots! Hell, I reckon Clinton and Farris have made a mess of busting the jail.'

'They looked like a couple of no-hopers to me,' Dunne observed.

'Clinton is the sensible one, but

sometimes Farris gets out of control.' Parker listened to the fading echoes of the shooting. 'I'd better take a look outside and see what's going on.'

'Do you want me to go with you?' Dunne asked.

'The hell I do! Your face is too well known around here. Just sit tight. I'll have another bottle brought in to you. I won't be more than a few minutes.'

Parker left the office and went into the saloon. He told the bartender to take a fresh bottle of whiskey into the office. No one seemed to have heard the shots, and he crossed to the batwings and peered out around the street. The town was peaceful, but a dog was barking persistently somewhere along the street. A man approached, and Parker stepped aside to give him space to enter.

'I thought I heard shots,' Parker observed.

'Yeah, I heard them,' the man replied. 'But that's nothing new these days.'

Parker went out to the sidewalk and looked towards the law office, wondering what Farris and Clinton were doing. He walked along the sidewalk, and stepped into an alley when he saw a man open the law office door and enter. He hurried along to the alley beside the law office and faded into the shadows to make for the alley window. When he looked into the office he saw Farris lying on the floor with Doc Errol bending over him. He studied the big man who was standing over Farris with a drawn gun, and recognized him as the man called Blaine, who had shot Ben Hussey in the saloon the night Hussey had tried to set up Billy Ormond.

It looked as if Blaine had been in the law office when Farris and Clinton made their play. Parker turned instantly and hurried back to the saloon, intent on warning Dunne of the situation. He found the outlaw asleep on the couch in the office. The fresh bottle of whiskey was on the floor beside the couch. Parker suppressed a sigh. He shook Dunne's shoulder but there was no response. He took a pistol from a drawer in his desk, checked it, stuck it into his waistband, and then left the saloon by the back door.

Dense shadows shrouded the back lots but Parker moved unerringly through the night to enter the alley beside the law office. He peered through the alley window into the office and saw Hilt seated at the desk. Farris was still lying on the floor, and Parker wondered if the big man was dead. There was no sign of Doc Errol. Parker checked his pistol and then paused to listen intently. The town was silent now. He raised the gun, smashed the office window with the barrel, and emptied the weapon at Hilt.

Gun smoke obscured Parker's vision. When the hammer of the pistol struck an empty chamber he peered into the office. Hilt was no longer sitting at the desk. Parker, certain he had riddled Hilt, hastened away into the shadows and returned to his office.

Hilt had hurled himself to the floor when he heard the sound of breaking glass, and had barely left his seat when

154

a bullet smacked into the desk top. He fell on his left side and lay motionless as all hell broke loose. Pain flashed through the half-healed wound in his left arm as he hit the floor. Five shots blasted the office in quick succession. He heard the slugs splintering into the desk, but he was untouched by the lethal storm and, when the shooting ceased, he drew his Colt and pushed himself upright. He dropped into his seat, clenching his teeth against darting shafts of agony that enveloped his right thigh. Gun smoke drifted across the office. Hilt got wearily to his feet and limped to the alley window. He peered out but saw nothing, and resisted the impulse to give chase.

The office was thick with the stink of burned powder, and Hilt wondered what he had let himself in for by agreeing to take on the job of temporary law man. He checked the street door, and was not satisfied with its shattered fastening. He went into the cell block, jangling the bunch of keys.

Benton and Clinton were standing at the doors of their cells, gripping the bars, anxiety showing on their faces. Ben Hussey was lying on his back on his bunk, his eyes closed, but Hilt did not think the gambler was asleep. Clinton grimaced when he saw Hilt, apparently unharmed, and turned away from the door to sit on his bunk.

'What was all the shooting about out there?' Clinton demanded.

'One of your friends, no doubt, hoping to kill me,' Hilt replied. 'Who put you up to come busting in here tonight?'

Clinton shrugged. He stretched out on the bunk and closed his eyes. Hilt went back to the office, aware that he would get no information from these men. Someone knocked on the street door and Hilt drew his gun and crossed to it. He stood to one side as he called a challenge, and Doc Errol replied.

'I've got a carpenter with me, Hilt, and a couple of men to help me take Farris over to my place. Let me in.'

Hilt opened the door. Errol came into the office followed by a small, dark-haired man who was carrying a canvas bag that held the tools of his trade. Two townsmen entered and stood on the threshold.

'This is Jake Abbott,' Errol said. 'He'll put another lock on the door. What was the shooting, Hilt?'

'Someone stuck a gun through the alley window and cut loose at me,' Hilt replied.

'And he missed you?' Errol asked incredulously.

'I heard the window break, and was hitting the floor before the first shot was fired. He was gone by the time I got to the window.' Hilt sat down at the desk again and stretched his right leg out in an attempt to ease the pain.

'There will be two townsmen coming in here on duty in the morning,' Errol informed him. 'I guess you'll want to get out after Dunne as soon as you can. I'll arrange for them to be relieved by two others around noon. That's the best

I can do at short notice. Every one is shocked by what happened to the sheriff and the posse men, but they'll recover in a day or two, and will rally round. I've spoken to Mayor Hartford about you taking over as a temporary law man and he is all for it. He'll swear you in tomorrow morning, and then you'll be all set.'

Hilt nodded. 'I think Dunne is the cause of all the trouble you're getting around here.' he mused, 'and it wouldn't surprise me to learn that he's got contacts in town — men who give him information or take an active part in some of his lawlessness.'

Errol heaved a sigh. 'That's about the weight of it,' he agreed. 'And Vince Parker, who owns the Black Ace saloon, is probably the kind of man Dunne would associate with. Two of Parker's employees came in here tonight with the intention of freeing Ben Hussey, and probably Benton. It might pay to investigate Parker.'

'After I've nailed Buck Dunne,' Hilt said firmly.

158

'You've got a free hand in the way you handle your new job. I wish you luck.' Errol turned to the two waiting townsmen. 'Let's get Farris over to my office and I'll take the bullet out of him.'

When Farris had been carried away, the carpenter began working on the shattered lock. Hilt sat at the desk, remaining motionless while a new lock was fitted to the door. His thoughts turned over the situation as he watched the carpenter, who quickly replaced the broken lock and then turned his attention to the shattered alley window.

'I can fit a square piece of wood in the aperture temporarily,' he said, 'and put in a new pane of glass tomorrow, if that's all right by you.'

'That'll be fine,' Hilt replied.

Abbott measured the aperture. 'I'll have to fetch a piece of wood. I'll be back in a few minutes.'

'I'll lock the door while you're gone,' Hilt said. 'Knock when you get back.'

The carpenter departed and Hilt

locked the door. He paced the office, impatient for sunup, when he could set out once more to hunt for Buck Dunne, and he vowed that this time nothing would prevent him from avenging the death of his brother.

7

Vince Parker was elated as he returned to his office; certain that his fusillade of shots had killed his intended victim. He went into the bar and helped himself to a whiskey. Four men were seated at a corner table, playing poker. He caught the eye of one of them, Jabe Montell, and nodded imperceptibly towards the rear door which gave access to his office. When he walked through to the back, Montell threw in his hand and got up from the table to follow. He entered Parker's office to find the saloon man seated at his desk. Buck Dunne was snoring, dead to the world, on the couch.

'It's all right for some, Boss.' Montell observed. He was of Mexican descent, swarthy-featured, with brown eyes that glittered in the lamplight. Black hair showed under the brim of his Stetson.

He was wearing range clothes although he rarely visited the range. His hands were soft — more suited to a pistol than a lariat — and he did illicit part-time jobs that kept plenty of money rattling in his pockets.

'He's had a bad day,' Parker observed.

'Yeah, I saw his gang come out of the bank this morning. It was bad luck Ike Prescott was standing nearby with that guy who pulled the Ormonds out of their trouble.'

'Do you know that guy by sight?' Parker's interest quickened. He glanced at the snoring Dunne. 'All I know about him is that his name is Frank Blaine. They say he came into the county trailing Dunne for killing his brother.'

Montell nodded. 'I was in the saloon the night Hussey was setting up Billy Ormond when Blaine came in and shot Hussey in the shoulder. I never saw a faster draw. So why is Dunne sleeping when the man who wants to kill him is shooting the hell out of his gang?'

'Buck ain't aware that Blaine is that

close to him. But I reckon Blaine is dead now. Take a look along the street and find out what's happening at the law office. I want to know if Blaine has cashed his chips.'

'Do you want me to kill him if he ain't?'

'Do you think you can?'

'I wouldn't call him out face to face.' Montell grimaced. 'I ain't ready for boot hill just yet. A bullet in the back would be better. I'd pick my time and give it to him right between the shoulder blades.'

'That sounds like a good idea.' Parker nodded. 'There's a hundred bucks in it for you if Blaine is put down for good.'

'That's easy money!' Montell hitched up his holstered pistol and turned to the door.

Parker watched him depart, and then picked up the whiskey bottle by the couch and poured himself a large drink.

Montell discovered several men standing in front of the law office. The street door was closed; shadows were dense on the sidewalk and the men gathered there were talking excitedly. Montell listened intently, and learned that a temporary sheriff had been appointed and someone had tried to kill him.

'Who is the new sheriff?' asked Montell.

'Blaine, who helped out the Ormonds when they were in trouble,' someone said. 'He was on the street when Buck Dunne and his gang rode in this morning, and he sure shot the hell out of them. Now he's taken over as sheriff, and someone emptied a pistol through the alley window at him.'

'Is he dead?' Montell queried.

'No. Doc Errol came out a few moments ago and said Blaine is sitting at the desk in there, waiting for the next attack. He must have more lives than a cat.'

'Pete Maxwell wasn't so lucky,' someone observed. 'Do they know who shot him?'

'Pete wasn't a gun hand,' another replied. 'He was out of his depth in that job. But who is doing all the shooting?'

Montell stepped into the shadows of the alley beside the office and remained motionless until the townsmen lost interest in the situation and drifted away. Then he walked along the alley to the side widow only to discover that the shattered pane of glass had been replaced by a rectangular board. He pressed his hand against the board, and when it did not budge he returned to the alley mouth, eased around the corner, and peered into the office through the front window. The lower panes of glass were covered with a patterned glass paper and he had to stand on tip-toe to peer through a clear pane. He could see an end of the desk but nothing of the new sheriff, so eased back into the alley and stood waiting patiently.

Inside the office, Hilt sat at the desk, his pistol lying on the desk top ready to hand. He felt restless. Again he found himself pushed into a situation he did not care for. He would rather have been out at Diamond O, for Sue was all alone out there with a dead brother and a badly wounded father, and Buck Dunne was somewhere around. The pungent smell of gun smoke lingered in the office, and seemed to cling in his throat. He got up suddenly, unable to sit easy with so much on his mind. Pain stabbed through his leg and he clenched his teeth. He promised himself that come the morning he would ride out to pick up Dunne's trail, and nothing would sidetrack him.

There was no sound in the office. He sat down again and picked up his pistol. Time was hanging heavily on his hands. He glanced at the big clock on a wall of the office and realized he had four hours before sunup. He was tired and needed sleep, but with unknown men in the town trying to shoot him he knew he would be unable to relax his alertness.

He got up again, picked up the bunch of keys, unlocked the door leading into the cells, and went to the back door to check that it was securely locked. He turned down the lamp burning in the cell block. The prisoners were silent and still on their bunks. One of them was snoring. Hilt went back into the office and eased into his seat at the desk; the morning could not come quickly enough for him. He propped his injured leg on another chair in an attempt to ease the throbbing pain nagging in it. As the minutes passed, his pain eased and he closed his eyes and dozed fitfully.

Montell stood in the alley until his patience was exhausted. When he realized that he would not be able to get to his intended victim until morning he gave up his vigil and went back to the saloon to report to Parker.

'I've been waiting for the shooting,' Parker said. 'When you didn't come back to report Blaine's death I figured he was still alive and you were laying for him. So what's going on?'

'He's still alive,' Montell explained. 'You didn't even wound him. He's got the alley window boarded up, and when

I looked through the front window of the office he had moved the desk so he can't be seen from the front. I'm gonna have to wait until he shows on the street in the morning to get a clear shot at him.'

'The hell you say!' Parker shook his head. 'I want him dead before sunup! If you're scared to tackle him on your own then get a couple of men — take six to back you up. Smash the front window of the office, blast the inside until you kill him, and then fade away into the night. We don't want any witnesses to the killing so get it done pronto.'

'OK, Boss. I'll get hold of Fargo, Brazos, and a couple more. They'll back me in this.'

'And, when you have killed Blaine,' Parker continued, 'get in that office and free the prisoners. Hussey is in there, and Clinton and Benton.'

Montell nodded and departed once more. He went through the saloon, found Fargo Watson playing poker, and beckoned him out of the game. Fargo, short and fat, joined Montell at the bar. He was overweight and his chest wheezed as he breathed. He wore a six-gun in a tied down holster on his left hip.

'Whaddya want?' Watson demanded. 'I had a winning hand when you came in — the first one all night.'

'We've got a job to do,' Montell said. 'Where's Brazos? We'll need him and three more of the boys along.'

'All of us? Who do you want killed? Or are we gonna rob a bank?'

'Frank Blaine is in the law office. He's taken over as the new sheriff. We've got to kill him and free the prisoners in the jail.'

'Jeez! No wonder you want half a dozen guns! Blaine is a one-man army! He killed just about everyone lined up against the Ormonds.'

'Hit him in the right place with a bullet and he'll go down like any other man,' Montell sneered. 'I'll wait here while you get the others. Bring them in for a drink before we start the job.'

Watson departed. Montell asked for a whiskey and gulped it quickly. Minutes later, the gunman called Brazos shouldered his way through the batwings and came to his side.

'Fargo said you want me,' Brazos demanded. 'Can't it wait until morning?'

'Shut up and get yourself a drink. What we have to do won't take long. We'll get moving as soon as the others show up.'

'It's a big job then.'

'Big enough!' Montell poured another whiskey from the bottle the bartender had left in front of him. He was on his third drink when Fargo appeared at the batwings, followed by two other men, Shurrock and Pierce. 'One drink each, boys,' Montell said, 'and then we'll get moving.'

They drank quickly. Montell led the way out to the sidewalk.

'What's the job?' Shurrock demanded.

'We're gonna bust open the jail,'

Montell said, 'by smashing the big front window and shooting the hell out of the new sheriff. When he's dead we'll get his keys, open the cells, and turn the prisoners loose.'

They made no comment as they walked along the sidewalk. Montell checked his surroundings. The street was deserted, and the lights in most of the buildings along the street had been extinguished. He slowed the pace as they neared the law office. Dim lamp light showed at the front window. He motioned for his crew to halt and went forward alone to peer through the window. Silence and darkness pressed in around him. He risked a glance through the window: the office seemed deserted. He could see an end of the desk and edged to his right to bring more of it into view. When he could see at least half of the chair behind the desk he realized that it was vacant: there was no sign of the new sheriff.

Montell looked around the office and noted that the door leading into the cell block was ajar. Blaine was obviously checking his prisoners. He eased back from the window and beckoned his men forward.

'Brazos, find a crate, or something heavy and smash the window when I give the word. The rest of you start shooting as soon as the glass shatters. When Blaine goes down, we stop shooting and, Shurrock, you get through the window and unlock the street door so we can get into the office. Then, Pierce, you grab the cell keys and get the prisoners out. Once they are free we beat it out the back door of the jail and leg it back to the saloon. Do it like that and it'll go OK.'

Brazos moved away and Montell looked into the office, gun in hand and ready for action. There was no sign of Blaine. He waited patiently for the new sheriff to put in an appearance. Brazos returned lugging a wooden crate.

Hilt stood in the cell block. An unnatural sound had disturbed him and he looked into the cells holding the prisoners to ensure that they were asleep and secure. Hussey was lying on his back with his hat over his face to shield his eyes from the lamplight, and it was difficult to tell if the gambler was sleeping or awake, but he was motionless and breathing steadily. Clinton was curled up on his right side, obviously asleep; Patton was asleep in a sitting position on his bunk, and Benton was lying on his back with his hands under his head. He was awake, and stared at Hilt impassively, his expression sullen.

Hilt tried the doors of the cells and then turned his attention to the back door, which was locked and bolted. Satisfied that all was well, he limped back to the front office, and, as he pushed the connecting door wide open, Hoagy Benton called to him.

'I could do with a drink of water, lawman.'

Hilt paused in the open doorway. He had noticed a bucket of water standing on a small table in the cell block with a dipper beside it, and turned abruptly to attend to Benton. As he moved, there was an almighty crash at the street end of the office and he jerked his head around to see the front window shattering. His reflexes were such that he was diving to one side back into the cell block when a shot hammered and a bullet smacked into the doorway where he had been standing. The next instant a deluge of pistol fire hammered and rolled thunderously. Splinters flew out of the woodwork around the doorway. Hilt felt a vicious tug at his right boot as a bullet struck his heel. His dive carried him away from the doorway, and he cursed as fresh pain stabbed through his right thigh when he struck it against the ground. He rolled and flattened out as he clawed at his pistol. The big weapon slid out of its holster and he cocked it.

The storm of lead continued unabated as Hilt squirmed around to face the doorway. His brain seemed bludgeoned by the strident cacophony. He lay with his body pressed flat to the ground.

Splinters of wood flew from the door and fell around him as he removed his Stetson and eased forward until he could peer into the office at ground level. He saw gun flashes at the window, and spotted a figure in the act of leaping in over the windowsill. Bullets clanged and jangled against the bars of the cell opposite the open door, and a ricochet buzzed closely over Hilt's head before plunking into the water bucket on the table. Gun smoke drifted in a pungent cloud across the office.

Hilt saw the street door open. The man who opened it was silhouetted momentarily in the doorway and Hilt fired. The man staggered and fell. Another man rushed in through the doorway from the sidewalk, his pistol hammering, but all his shots were aimed waist high, and Hilt was down on the floor. Hilt fired again. The man went down in a skidding fall and remained motionless.

The shooting from the shattered front window increased as the attackers endeavoured to silence Hilt's deadly gun, and shots were now directed at his position on the floor. He eased back and stood up. His right leg throbbed painfully; he wondered remotely if it would ever have the opportunity to heal. Flashes ripped the shadows apart and the guns continued in a desperate drum roll of fire. The attackers certainly meant to nail him! At least five guns had started the shooting, and the survivors sounded as if they were getting desperate to finish him.

Hilt risked a glance around the door jamb, and pulled back when a slug crackled past his face so close he imagined he could feel its heat. He leaned against the inside of the wall beside the door and lifted his right foot from the ground. Moments later the shooting seemed to ease, and then it cut out altogether and echoes faded sullenly. Hilt peered into the office again. A cloud of gun smoke was drifting across his view, pungent and sickening. He squinted to pierce the gloom. One of the first shots had struck the lamp on the desk and extinguished it.

The attackers had apparently pulled out. One man was lying inertly on the threshold and another lay crumpled across the doorstep. Hilt remained motionless, covering the open door and the broken window. He realized that a raid such as this had to succeed instantly, before townsmen could arrive to investigate the shooting, and he had stopped the assailants dead in their tracks. He wondered who was so keen to break out his prisoners. He waited, aware that time was on his side, and the ensuing silence seemed to hurt his ears more than the shooting had done.

'Hilt, are you in there?' A voice which Hilt recognized as Doc Errol's called from just outside the street door.

'I'm here, Doc.' Hilt eased forward, his gun steady in his right hand. He limped across the office, paused to check the man lying on the floor, and continued when he found his assailant dead.

Errol moved into the doorway and

examined the man lying huddled there.

'This one is dead,' Errol commented. 'What the devil happened, Hilt?'

Hilt explained in a steady tone. Errol cursed.

'I'll get some light on the scene,' Errol said. 'We need to see who was doing the shooting.'

'I'm wondering about that,' Hilt mused. He stood with his gun covering the doorway while the doctor moved around him. A match scraped and dim light flared. Errol tried to relight the office lamp but a bullet had smashed the oil reservoir which had drained. He edged into the cell block and picked up the lamp burning there. When he returned to Hilt's side and held the lamp over the dead man lying on the threshold he muttered an imprecation and looked up at Hilt.

'This is Dave Shurrock,' Errol said sharply. He moved to the doorway and thrust the lamp towards the second dead man's upturned face. 'And this is Jack Pierce.'

178

'Who were they when they were up and shooting?' Hilt demanded.

'They worked for Vince Parker, who owns the Black Ace saloon. He has a number of disreputable men working for him.'

'Is that so? That's interesting. Clinton and Farris are Parker's men. I guess I'll have to talk to Parker. I reckon he'll know why his men have been attacking the law office.'

There was a noise at the street door and Hilt spun around, his gun lifting. Two townsmen were peering into the office, one of them holding a shotgun.

'Joe,' said Errol, 'you're just in time to stand guard in here while the sheriff and I take a walk along the street to do some checking up. There are prisoners in the cells, and we want to find them still here when we get back. Come on in and lock the door after we leave.'

'I ain't a lawman, Doc,' Joe Mountjoy replied, edging away.

'And neither am I,' Errol countered, 'but I find myself helping the law department at the moment, and I'm sure you have the same sentiments I do. Come on in, Joe. We shan't be more than a few minutes. Just hold the fort until we return.'

Joe Mountjoy entered the office, still protesting. Hilt reloaded the empty chambers of his pistol. He handed Mountjoy the keys to the cells.

'Don't go near the prisoners,' he said firmly. 'They are dangerous men.'

Mountjoy nodded, took the keys, and dumped them on a corner of the desk. He sat down on the chair behind the desk, still gripping his shotgun, and looked around uneasily.

Hilt limped out to the sidewalk, intent on carrying the fight to those men who were ranged against the law. He was filled with impatience because he wanted to get after Dunne . . .

*   *   *

Fleeing from the law office, Montell led Fargo and Brazos along an alley to the back lots and thence to the Black Ace saloon. The rear door to the saloon was barred so Montell traversed an alley to the street and they entered the saloon through the batwings.

'Get a drink,' Montell suggested to his companions. 'I'll talk to Parker.'

Brazos and Fargo needed no urging. They bellied up to the bar.

Parker was pacing his office like a caged mountain lion. Buck Dunne was awake and seated on the couch, his pistol in his hand. Parker turned quickly to confront Montell when the office door opened.

'Well?' Parker demanded.

'It was no dice, Boss.' Montell said. 'We got into the office but Blaine was too good for us. Shurrock and Pierce went down and the rest of us couldn't get a clear shot at Blaine. I allowed myself three minutes to open the jail and get the prisoners out, but Blaine held us off and we had to beat it out of there before any townsfolk showed up. That lawman fights like a one-man army!'

Parker cursed. 'Did you leave Shurrock and Pierce back at the jail?' he demanded.

Montell shrugged. 'There was no way we could get them out of there. We had a tough chore getting away ourselves.'

'So two men who are known to work for me are lying dead along the street for anyone to recognize, and earlier Farris and Clinton were caught trying to bust open the jail! Where the hell do you think that puts me, Montell? I'm right behind the eight-ball! Jeez! We'll have Blaine walking in here any minute to ask questions.'

'That's OK by me,' Dunne interposed. 'I've been hoping to meet up with Blaine.'

'Well, I don't want to meet him,' Parker opened a cupboard and picked up a couple of saddle-bags. 'I'm getting out of here for a spell, and you'd better make yourself scarce too, Buck.' He put some ledgers in the saddle bags, and then opened the safe in a corner and took out a large quantity of paper money. 'I'll head out to the Downey ranch for a few days. Montell, take over here, and, if anyone shows up asking for me, tell them I went out to the ranch early this morning. That should clear me around here. In the meantime, if you get a chance of shooting Blaine then take it, and don't miss him again. Come on, Buck, let's get the hell out of here before there is a showdown with the law.'

Dunne's face expressed reluctance as he followed Parker out of the office and into a barn out back. Parker saddled his chestnut and fixed the saddle bags behind the cantle. Dunne collected his mount and they rode off into the night, heading for Parker's new ranch . . .

8

Hilt and Doc Errol walked along the sidewalk to the Black Ace saloon. Small groups of men were standing around on the street, discussing the shooting. Hilt kept his right hand close to the butt of his holstered pistol; Doc Errol had armed himself with a double-barrelled shotgun before leaving the law office. When they reached the batwings of the saloon, Hilt paused.

'You don't have to come in here with me, Doc,' he said. 'I reckon I can handle any trouble that might come up.'

'Someone has got to back you,' said Errol firmly.

'OK. So just follow my lead. You'll be able to identify Parker's men for me. Don't stand too close to me in here in case there is shooting.'

'I'll be right behind you,' Errol said tensely.

Hilt peered over the batwings. He saw a bartender talking to two customers as he shouldered his way through the swing doors. The 'tender glanced in Hilt's direction when he heard the batwings creak, and then, at the sight of the law badge on Hilt's shirt front, slid one hand out of sight under the bar. The two men at the bar jerked their heads around, and both dropped their hands to their holstered guns as if expecting trouble. Hilt paused at the nearest corner of the bar, his right hand close to the butt of his pistol.

'Get your hands clear of your guns,' Hilt rasped. 'I'm hair-triggered!' He paused until the three men at the bar obeyed his command. 'Now let us talk,' he continued. 'Bartender, has anyone come in here in the last few minutes?'

'Not a soul. Sheriff,' the 'tender replied. He stood with both hands in plain view on the bar top, his sweating palms pressed against the polished surface. Beads of sweat appeared on his forehead like spots of rain on a window.

'What was all the shooting about?' His tone had gone up a couple of notches, and when he grinned it was merely a travesty of the real thing.

A door towards the back of the saloon banged and Hilt glanced around to see a man emerging through a rear doorway.

'That's Jabe Montell,' Doc Errol said in Hilt's ear. 'He runs things around here when Parker is out of town on business, and he's an undesirable, like these two men standing here drinking. They all work for Parker.'

'Montell, where is Vince Parker?' Hilt asked, as Montell came towards the bar.

'He rode out of town this morning and won't be back until some time tomorrow, so he told me before he left,' Montell replied. 'Is there something I can do for you?'

'Maybe you can. Where has Parker gone?'

'He didn't tell me that. All I know is that he had some business out of town to take care of.'

'And you've been in here all evening?' Hilt queried.

'Sure. That's my job,' Montell countered. 'Will you have a drink with me? The boss likes to be on a friendly footing with the local law.'

Hilt palmed his gun and cocked it as he thrust the muzzle over the top of the bar.

'Just stand still, all of you,' he commanded. 'Several men attacked the law office a few minutes ago and shot the hell out of the place — perhaps you heard the shooting! So I want to check your guns to see if they have been fired recently. Get your hands up while Doc Errol checks out your hardware.'

'I just told you I've been in here all evening,' Montell protested. 'And these two have been on duty since noon.'

'Then you won't mind me checking your guns,' Hilt persisted. 'Get your hands up shoulder high and keep your mouths shut.'

Fargo and Brazos lifted their hands immediately, their expressions identical:

both filled with shock. Montell remained motionless, his hand close to the
butt of his gun, and he seemed intent
on confronting Hilt. But Doc Errol
eased around Hilt and lifted his
shotgun to cover all three men.

'Just do like the sheriff tells you,
Montell,' Errol said. 'I've never shot a
man, and I don't want to start now, so
get on with it.'

Hilt saw the bartender surreptitiously
inching his right hand back to the edge
of the bar as if intent on reaching
beneath it for a hidden weapon. He
squeezed his trigger, filling the saloon
with gun thunder that set glasses
rattling on the back bar. The bullet
struck the 'tender's right hand before
tearing a long sliver of wood out of the
bar top and ricocheting to clang against
the big pot-bellied stove towards the
rear of the long room. The bartender
jumped about a foot in the air,
screeched in pain, and grasped his
shattered hand as blood spurted.

'Let's get on with it,' Hilt rapped as

the gun echoes faded.

Montell lifted his hands quickly. His dark eyes glittered as he gazed at Hilt. Doc Errol laid his shotgun on the bar close to Hilt and skirted the three men. He removed Montell's pistol from its holster, sniffed the muzzle, and then nodded.

'This gun has been fired recently,' he observed. He put the weapon on the bar and moved around Brazos.

'I fired my gun this morning.' Brazos said as Doc Errol relieved him of his pistol. 'I shot a rat in the stable when I went for my horse.'

'It has been fired recently,' Errol confirmed.

Fargo stood motionless until Doc Errol moved between him and Hilt's gun, but the instant he was masked by Errol's body Brazos grabbed the doctor, his arm snaking around Errol's neck. He swung Errol around as a shield against Hilt, his right hand lifting to the butt of Errol's pistol, which was protruding from the waistband of the doctor's pants. Hilt moved quickly, as if controlled by Fargo's brain. He stepped to his left, putting Montell between himself and the pistol Fargo was bringing into action. Montell moved backwards a couple of quick steps to get out of the line of fire.

Hilt saw Montell's right hand drop to the back of his neck, and paused for the briefest moment. Montell pulled a knife from a sheath down between his shoulder blades.

Hilt fired a shot as Montell jerked his hand to throw the knife; his foresight was pointed at Montell's belly. The gun blasted and Montell jerked as if he had been kicked by a mule. He bent forward at the waist, his knife spinning to the floor, and he followed the blade down in a slack, almost lazy movement, blood spurting from the gaping wound in his abdomen.

Gun smoke drifted. Hilt aggravated the wound in his right leg as he lunged to his right in an effort to draw a bead on Fargo, who was out of sight behind

Doc Errol, now struggling to get away from the gunman's grasp. Brazos was leaning forward to snatch Montell's pistol off the bar where Errol had placed it. Out of a corner of his eye, Hilt noted the bartender reaching under the bar for a weapon.

Hilt fired at the gun Brazos was reaching for. His slug sent the weapon skittering along the bar out of reach. Brazos turned and dropped to his hands and knees, attempting to scoop up the knife Montell had discarded. Hilt turned his pistol on the bartender as the man lifted a sawn-off shotgun into view. He fired a single shot, saw a splotch of blood appear on the bartender's shirt front, and swung his gun to cover Brazos as he came up with the knife in his hand. Doc Errol had got a hand to Fargo's wrist and was trying desperately to wrest the weapon from the gunman's grasp.

Brazos came erect and swung his right hand in a fast arc to throw the knife at Hilt, but saw in that instant that he was too slow. Hilt's pistol lifted a fraction. Brazos saw the weapon flame and smoke; heard the crash of the shot. He felt a flashing pain in his chest, as if he had been struck by lightning. His brain barely had time to register agony before a black curtain slipped before his eyes and he fell in a lifeless heap.

Hilt went forward, trying to favour his right leg. Doc Errol had forced Fargo's gun hand upwards so that the weapon was pointing toward the ceiling, but he was not strong enough to wrest the gun from Fargo's grasp. Hilt swung his pistol and crashed the long barrel against the back of Fargo's head. The gunman groaned, dropped his gun, and fell to the floor. Errol reeled against the bar, gasping for breath.

'Are you OK, Doc?' Hilt demanded as he took stock of the situation.

'I am now!' Errol replied. He straightened and picked up Fargo's pistol to sniff at the muzzle. 'It has been fired recently,' he said, and turned to examine Brazos. 'He's dead,' he commented, and moved to where Montell was lying. 'Montell is dead also. That was mighty fine shooting, Hilt.'

'It's the only way to stay alive,' Hilt replied. 'Kill or be killed!' He glanced over the bar to look at the 'tender lying on the floor behind it. 'It looks like three out of four are dead. Maybe Fargo will talk when he comes round. But there's little doubt that these men took part in the attack on the law office.'

'Which brings Vince Parker into it,' Errol mused. 'I wonder where he's gone.'

'We'll get around to him before long,' Hilt promised.

Doc Errol went behind the bar and examined the bartender. 'You're right,' he commented. 'He's dead. Would you like a drink, Hilt? I could sure do with something strong after that business.'

'Not for me, thanks.' Hilt turned to the insensible Fargo, bent to grasp him by his shirt, and shook the heavy body.

Fargo groaned. His eyelids flickered, and then opened. He gazed uncomprehendingly at Hilt for several moments before awareness seeped into his eyes. 'On your feet,' Hilt commanded, and Fargo scrambled to his feet and leaned on the bar.

Errol came around the bar with a whiskey in his hand. He gulped a mouthful of the fiery liquid before handing the glass to Fargo, who took it eagerly. Hilt waited until Fargo set down the empty glass. The gunman straightened and looked around, his expression hardening when he saw Montell and Brazos stretched out on the floor.

'You've killed them!' Fargo exclaimed.

'They could have taken the easy way,' Hilt replied. 'They didn't have to resist. From their actions, I take it that they attacked the jail, and you were with them.'

'I don't know a thing about that.' Fargo shook his head.

'So let us go along to the law office,'

Hilt persisted. 'I'll put you behind bars until you decide to tell the truth.'

He motioned to the batwings with his pistol. Fargo grimaced and staggered forward. Doc Errol picked up his shotgun and followed behind. Hilt was not pleased. He preferred prisoners to corpses, for dead men told no tales, and without proof the guilty could go free.

* * *

Joe Mountjoy sat in the law office listening to Hilt and Doc Errol departing along the sidewalk. When the sound of their footsteps faded he put down his shotgun and got up from the desk. Barely pausing to grab the bunch of cell keys, he hurried into the cell block. Clinton lifted his head to see who had entered, and when he recognized Mountjoy he got up off his bunk and came to the barred door of his cell.

'What are you doing in here, Joe?' Clinton demanded.

Mountjoy grinned. 'I got roped in to guard the prisoners until the new sheriff comes back,' he said. 'Now ain't that a laugh? And I came along here hoping to be able to bust you out after I heard what happened to you and Farris.'

'How about opening the cell door, Joe?' Clinton was seized by a terrible impatience. He was afraid that Blaine would show up before he could get away. 'Something tells me it is time to call it quits around here. Open up quick. I'll pick up some dough from Parker and hit the trail for other parts. I ain't a fool. I can tell which way the wind is blowing. It looks like I'm finished around here.'

'I'll ride with you,' said Mountjoy. 'Anyway, the pickings around here have got mighty slim lately.' He unlocked the door of Clinton's cell. 'What about these others?'

'Turn them all loose,' Clinton instructed. 'I'll look in the office for a gun.' He hurried into the front office.

Mountjoy unlocked the other cells and the prisoners went into the front office to arm themselves. Hussey paused and looked at Mountjoy.

'Where is Blaine?' Hussey demanded.

'He's gone to the Black Ace to bring in the men who were shooting up this place.'

Hussey hastened into the office. Clinton was buckling a gunbelt around his waist. Benton took a Winchester off a rack on the back wall of the office and then pulled open a drawer in the desk to look for cartridges.

'We'd better leave by the back door in case Blaine is on the street,' Clinton said. 'I'm heading for the livery barn. The sooner I'm on a horse the better I shall like it.' He checked the pistol he had acquired, thrust it back into his holster, and grasped Mountjoy's arm. 'Come on, Joe, it is time to make tracks.'

Mountjoy led the way to the back door, unlocked it, and threw down the bunch of keys. He and Clinton slipped away into the darkness of the alley, followed a moment later by Benton and Patton. Hussey found a pistol in a drawer of the desk, checked that it was loaded, and started for the back door. He took a couple of steps before pausing, and then turned and headed for the street door. He was not inclined to run. Blaine had shot him a month ago and he wanted revenge. He unlocked the street door and stepped out to the sidewalk, gun in hand. He looked around the deserted street, and then concealed himself in the shadows of the nearest alley.

Fargo, holding his hands shoulder high, walked towards the law office with Hilt in close attendance. Doc Errol followed behind Hilt, who was holding his gun. The town was quiet now; the townsmen who had been disturbed by the shooting were beginning to drift away. Hilt did not relax his vigilance. He peered into the surrounding darkness, ready for any eventuality.

He caught a faint shifting of the

dense shadows at the alley mouth beside the law office as Fargo drew level with it, and heard a slight, unnatural noise. Reacting without conscious thought, Hilt stepped in close to the shop front at the corner of the alley, crouching in an effort to silhouette anyone waiting in ambush. Fargo halted in mid-stride and uttered an imprecation as a figure pushed out of the alley and almost collided with him.

'Fargo?' Ben Hussey demanded. 'Is that you?'

'Hussey!' Fargo ejaculated. 'How'd you get out of jail?'

Hilt was shielded by Fargo, and Hussey had not seen him, but the gambler saw that Fargo had his hands up. He twisted back into the alley mouth; he missed seeing Hilt's figure pressed against the shop doorway, but he saw Doc Ellis.

'Hussey!' Doc said, overhearing Fargo's words. He reached for the pistol stuck in his waistband.

Hilt levelled his gun. He could just

make out Hussey's head and shoulders in the alley mouth.

'Get your hands up, Hussey,' Hilt rapped. 'I've got you covered.'

Hussey swung his pistol towards Hilt but Fargo was in his line of fire.

'Get the hell out of the way, Fargo,' Hussey cursed.

Hilt sprang away from the front of the shop. Fargo was between him and Hussey. Hilt crossed the sidewalk, jarring his right leg painfully as he did so. He fell off the sidewalk as he moved to his right, and landed on his knees in the dust of the street. His view of the alley opened up. He saw Hussey drawing a bead on him, but Fargo was partially in the line of fire and Hussey's aim was balked.

Hilt triggered his gun. He was able to see Hussey's head above and behind Fargo's, and aimed a couple of inches above Fargo's hat. His gun blasted and orange flame spurted. Fargo dropped to the sidewalk and lay still. Hilt blinked rapidly, trying to pierce the gun dazzle that blinded him momentarily. He knew his shot had missed Fargo by a fraction of an inch and fancied that he had hit Hussey. The gambler's movements had become erratic. He lost his grip on the weapon and sagged back against the corner of the alley, his knees buckling. Hilt prepared to fire a second shot, but suddenly Hussey fell forward on his face.

Fargo was cursing angrily. He pushed himself to his feet and put his hands shoulder high. Hilt got up, clenching his teeth against the darting pain in his leg. Doc Errol hurried forward and bent over the motionless Hussey; he kicked aside the gambler's discarded gun.

'An inch higher and you would have missed him, Hilt,' Errol confirmed. 'That was damned good shooting under the circumstances.'

'You nearly hit me,' Fargo protested. 'That slug almost parted my hair.'

'Think yourself lucky you're still alive,' Hilt responded. 'Let's get into the office pronto. I want to check on how Hussey got out of his cell.'

Fargo entered the office, his hands still shoulder high. Hilt covered the office with his gun, saw it was deserted, and wondered what had happened to Joe Mountjoy. He saw that the connecting door was ajar and motioned for Doc Errol to cover Fargo. He hastened into the cell block, his gun uplifted, and paused when he saw that all the cells were empty. The doors were open; the back door of the jail was wide open. There was no sign of Mountjoy, but the bunch of cell keys lay on the floor by the cell that had housed Hoagy Benton.

Fargo came into the cell block with Errol behind him.

Hilt motioned for the prisoner to enter a cell, and then picked up the bunch of keys and locked the door.

'Where is Mountjoy?' Errol demanded.

'You might well ask!' Hilt looked around. 'I told him not to bother with

202

the prisoners, but it looks like he came in here to look at them, and brought the cell keys with him.'

'Do you think he turned the prisoners loose, or did they get the better of him?' Errol queried.

'We'll ask him, if we ever see him again.' Hilt holstered his gun. 'It looks like Mountjoy left with the prisoners. I'll get along to the livery barn. Benton will need a horse. Perhaps you will stay here and take care of the place until I get back, Doc.'

Errol nodded. He went into the office and dropped wearily into the seat behind the desk. Hilt limped to the street door and then paused. He glanced back at the doctor, shook his head, and departed silently. Figures were appearing on the street again, attracted by the latest shots.

Hilt limped along the sidewalk towards the livery barn at the end of the street, followed by at least six curious townsmen. As he approached the doorway of the big barn he saw yellow lamplight issuing from it, and faded into the shadows to peer into the interior through an adjacent window. There was movement inside. He saw Mountjoy leading a horse to the rear door, and Clinton, already mounted, was in the act of disappearing into the darkness beyond the door.

Drawing his pistol, Hilt crashed the barrel through the window, shattering the pane of glass. Mountjoy swung round at the disturbance, his face frozen into a mask of shock. He was holding a pistol in his right hand, and pointed it in Hilt's direction as he sprang into the saddle of the horse he was leading. The pistol hammered. Hilt ducked as a slug thudded into the woodwork of the window frame. Mountjoy spurred the horse toward the back door. Hilt levelled his pistol as he shouted a warning.

'Hold it right there, Mountjoy, or you're a dead man!'

Mountjoy threw a glance over his shoulder. His mouth was gaping. He was either praying or cursing, his expression a mask of desperation. He fired a second shot in Hilt's direction as he dug his spurs into the flanks of the horse and ducked low in the saddle in a desperate effort to get through the rear doorway of the barn before Hilt could open fire. Hilt squeezed his trigger. His foresight was covering Mountjoy's shoulder blades. The gun blasted and gun smoke flew. Mountjoy jerked upright, half twisted to look back over his shoulder, and then slid out of his saddle and bounced on the hard packed ground. He remained motionless as the horse ran on into the blackness of the night.

Hilt exhaled sharply to rid his lungs of pungent gun smoke. He entered the barn and hastened to the back door. When he peered out for a sight of Benton and Clinton he saw no movement in the dense shadows. The sound of rapidly departing hoofs came to his ears, and faded almost at the instant he heard them. Silence ensued.

The echoes of the shooting were fading into the far distance. Joe Mountjoy lay motionless on the ground. Hilt shook his head and heaved a sigh. He went back to Mountjoy to check the man: Mountjoy was dead.

9

Hilt limped back to the law office with his ears ringing from the shock of the shooting. He paused at the Black Ace saloon and peered in over the batwings, attracted by the sound of voices. The bodies of Montell and Brazos were in the process of being removed by the town undertaker and an assistant. Hilt entered the big room and paused on the threshold. The undertaker, John Peck, a tall, thin, cadaverous-looking man, straightened from examining Montell and looked at Hilt.

'The place is closed,' Peck rasped. He saw the law badge on Hilt's shirt front and his expression changed. 'Vince Parker ain't around, and it looks like everyone who works for him is dead. There has been hell to pay tonight — nothing but shooting all over town. I can't keep up with it.'

'It's a good job I can,' Hilt replied. 'Have you noticed the bartender behind the bar? Take him as well and when you finish in here you'll find Joe Mountjoy dead in the livery barn. After that, you can pick up Ben Hussey from the sidewalk near the law office. I have a feeling you'll be finished for the night when you've done that.'

He departed and went on to the law office. Doc Errol was sitting behind the desk, his head in his hands. He looked up wearily when Hilt entered the office.

'I heard the shooting,' Errol said. 'Am I needed anywhere?'

Hilt shook his head. 'Not this time, Doc.' He explained the incident at the livery barn. 'I guess Mountjoy turned the prisoners loose. He was making a run for it on a horse when I got there, and I caught a glimpse of Clinton hoofing it. There was no sign of Benton.'

'Is there no end to this trouble?' Errol demanded, shaking his head. 'I thought it was all over when you killed

Sheriff Catlin a month ago. Maybe it was because you were laid low with your wounds that gave us the idea that it was done, but it resumed the minute you showed up in town again.'

Hilt nodded. 'We all thought it was over after that showdown, but you know what they say about a rotten apple in a barrel. So there were other badmen in town, and they are coming out of the woodwork now because they figure they are next on the list. And yet all I ever wanted to do was get Buck Dunne.' He uttered a short, bitter laugh. 'And even he showed up in town today to rob the bank. But he seems to have disappeared again after leaving Diamond O. I followed his hoof prints to town and then got caught up in all this trouble with Vince Parker's men.'

He sighed, removed the sheriff badge from his shirt, and tossed it on the desk. His face was impassive.

'What are you doing, Hilt?' Errol demanded.

'This isn't working out, Doc. I'm

knee-deep in action which is keeping me from what I came into the county to do. Apart from that, I'm stuck here in town when I should be at Diamond O. I feel pretty bad about Sue, out there alone with a badly hurt father and a dead brother on her hands. What must she be feeling at this moment? I'm quitting, Doc. As soon as I can I'm riding back to Diamond O to check with Sue, and if she is OK then I'll pick up Buck Dunne's trail in the morning and run him down. If nobody wants the sheriff's job then I can always come back here and handle it when Dunne is finished.'

'It looks like Vince Parker is the man behind this latest trouble,' Errol said heavily. 'As you say, all the shooting tonight was done by men who worked for him.'

'Parker left town this morning, so Montell said,' Hilt mused. 'Where could he have gone?'

'I've never known him to leave town before,' Errol replied, 'so perhaps there is some truth in the rumour that he bought Hank Downey's Big D spread when it came up for sale recently. Maybe that is where he has gone — to lie low until all this shooting is done.'

'Are you gonna be here all night?' Hilt asked.

'Sure, unless I get called out as a doctor. Why don't you hit the sack for a couple of hours? I'll wake you if I have to leave.'

'That sounds like a good idea.' Hilt stifled a yawn. 'I'll get my head down in a cell. I need to get the weight off my leg. Call me if you get any trouble.'

Hilt limped into the cell block leaving the connecting door open. Fargo was the only prisoner, and he was snoring when Hilt looked in on him. Hilt removed his cartridge belt and placed it with the butt of his pistol close to his head. He stretched out on the bunk and relaxed. His head was aching and darts of pain were stabbing through his right thigh. He sighed and closed his eyes wearily, thinking that he would not be able to sleep with so much on his mind, but exhaustion had taken its toll and he fell asleep almost immediately. It seemed only a few moments later when Doc Errol shook him awake, and he opened his eyes to see dawn lightening the barred window beside the back door.

'I figured you'd want to be on the trail early this morning,' Errol said. 'There's been no further trouble around here so it looks like you've shot the hell out of the opposition.'

'Thanks, Doc.' Hilt pushed himself to his feet. He eased his weight on to his right leg, felt a protest of pain, and picked up his gun belt. He buckled the heavy weapon around his waist. 'Can I borrow your buggy again today?'

'Sure. I'll get it for you if you'll stand by in here until I get back.'

Hilt nodded and went through to the front office. He sat down at the desk. The sheriff's badge was lying on the desk top where he had put it earlier and he picked it up, studied it, and then put it back on his shirt. Everything he had to do around here was exactly what a regular sheriff would be expected to handle. He stifled a yawn. He knew what he had to do, and was impatient to begin.

Doc Errol returned. He was looking tired. His face was pale but filled with determination. Hilt got to his feet.

'I'll be on my way, Doc,' he said. 'I'll go out to Diamond O and see how Sue is doing, and then look for Buck Dunne. I'll pick up Clinton and Benton if I see them on the trail, but Dunne is my priority. The others are just small fry. See you when I get back.'

'Good luck,' Errol responded. 'I hope you get Dunne.'

Hilt went out to the buggy and prepared to leave. A wave of relief filled him as he set out along the street. The town was silent and still and everything seemed normal as he departed. He took the trail to the Ormond ranch and sent the horse forward through the growing light of the new day. It was time he finished the hunt for Buck Dunne . . .

★ ★ ★

Vince Parker rode hard for the Big D ranch with Buck Dunne silent by his side. Parker was feeling increasingly worried at the way events had turned out back in town. He had always been most careful in his dealings with the lawless element that teemed and flourished in the remote areas and the back trails of the county, but his attempts to kill Blaine had gone wrong from the start, and now he suspected that the new sheriff would have put two and two together and worked out who was behind the abortive attempts that had been made against the jail.

He glanced sideways at the silent Dunne and came to the conclusion that under the present circumstances the gang boss was a liability; an embarrassment. Anyone seeing the two of them together would immediately assume that they were in cahoots. Parker experienced an impulse to shoot Dunne without warning, but shied away from the idea because he was afraid of making a hash of the attempt. But he had to clear himself in the eyes of the law. His employees could shoulder the blame for the attacks on the jail — he paid them to take such risks. If there was no proof against him personally then he would be well in the clear.

When they were nearing Diamond O, Parker reined in to give his horse a breather. He stepped down from his saddle and Dunne joined him.

'I've been thinking about what you said earlier, Buck,' said Parker.

'What did I say?' Dunne countered.

'That you want to take over Diamond O, and on second thoughts it might be a good idea. We're not far from Diamond O now, so why don't you ride in there and take a look around? If Chuck Ormond died there would only be the girl left, and she'll be easy to handle. You killed Billy Ormond, you said, so if the girl disappeared then the spread could fall into your hands with no trouble, and at a fraction of its market price.'

'That was what I was thinking,' Dunne said eagerly. 'I'll turn off there now and take a look around. I also need to get back to town and bust Benton out of jail. Then I'll have to recruit a new gang. And, like you say, Vince, if I kill Ormond and his daughter the place will come up for sale. You could handle that side of it for me, huh?'

'That's the idea!' Parker swung back into his saddle. 'I'll go on to my place to fix up an alibi. You do what you have to and I'll see you later.'

They parted. Parker rode on to Big D and Dunne headed for Diamond O.

Dunne was fired by the idea of becoming a cattle rancher. He wanted Diamond O; needed a respectable front for his lawless activities, and the fact that he would have to murder two people to get it did not cause him a moment of disquiet. He reached the huddle of buildings and reined in outside the yard to study the cow spread with narrowed eyes. There was

216

not a glimmer of light anywhere; the buildings were black and stark in the starlight. He wondered if the girl was awake — she would not get much sleep with her brother lying dead by the porch. He dismounted and led his horse around the edge of the yard to the corral and turned it into the enclosure.

He went to the barn and struck a match. A lantern was suspended from a post and he lighted it. He took a forkful of hay to the corral for his horse, and then fetched a bucket of water for the animal. With his chores done, he glanced at the sky and estimated that he had two hours to sunup. He was hungry, and went to the rear of the ranch house to get into the kitchen. The back door was unbolted and he entered noiselessly. He stood motionless for several moments, waiting until his eyes became accustomed to the black shadows. His ears were strained to pick up sound. The house was like the inside of a grave — dark and silent.

When he was satisfied that he had not disturbed anyone he lit a lamp in the kitchen and looked around for food. He found some cold beef on a plate in a cupboard and ate hungrily. He cut a thick slice of bread from a loaf and smeared it with butter. As he devoured the bread a faint sound alerted him and he swung round to face the inner kitchen door, his right hand dropping to the butt of his holstered gun. He stayed the movement when he saw Sue Ormond standing in the doorway holding a Winchester; its muzzle was pointing at his chest.

'It's you again!' Sue observed in a shocked tone. She had spent the hours since sundown sitting at a bedroom window overlooking the yard with a rifle in her hands, lost in a timeless void of grief, her distraught brain hammering endlessly the grim fact that her brother Billy was dead. She had wished many times during the seemingly endless hours of darkness that she might see Dunne again with a chance of killing him, and here he was, larger than life, ready for a single shot that would end his miserable existence. 'I'm going to kill you!' she said tonelessly. 'You made a big mistake by coming back.'

'Take it easy!' Dunne rasped. 'I've got this place surrounded by my gang. If you fire a shot they'll come busting in here like a herd of stampeding cattle and shoot everyone, including your pa. If you don't mind that then go ahead and shoot me, but if you want your pa to live then you'll put down that rifle and do like I say.'

'You're lying,' Sue replied calmly. 'I saw you ride up. You were alone. You put your horse in the corral and then came in here. I watched every movement you made, and you don't have a gang with you.' She lifted the muzzle of the rifle until it covered Dunne's heart. 'If you know any prayers then say them. You shot down my brother Billy, and I'll kill you for that.'

'Killing ain't a woman's chore,' Dunne ventured. 'Put down that rifle and I won't harm you.'

'I wouldn't trust you as far as I could push this house.' Sue laughed bitterly: a trace of hysteria sounded in her wavering tone. 'You killed Billy, and my father is lying badly wounded in his bed. Do you think I would trust you after what you have done?'

Dunne could see that she was beyond reason. The muzzle of the Winchester was aimed at his heart, and they were separated by a distance of six feet — too far for him to tackle her. He noted that the index finger of her right hand was tight against the trigger of the rifle and the weapon was not wavering. She seemed intent on killing him. He drew a deep breath and prepared for a life or death gamble. He had to distract her somehow and then disarm her.

'Your father is calling you,' he said, canting his head as if listening intently.

Sue half-turned her head to listen for sound, and he hurled himself forward to cover the short distance between them, his hands outstretched to grasp the rifle. Sue realized that he had tricked her and squeezed the trigger even as he grasped the barrel of the rifle to thrust it aside. The weapon exploded raucously. Dunne felt a lightning flash of pain in his left side, a stunning blow as his lower rib was broken. The impact of the 44.40 slug threw him backwards off his feet. He hit the floor hard, and, before his brain could register the grim fact that he had been shot, darkness more intense than midnight blacked out his vision and he slumped into unconsciousness.

* * *

Benton, Clinton, and Patton cleared Cedar Creek with gunfire ringing in their ears. Clinton caught up with Benton just outside of town.

'Where are you going?' Clinton demanded.

'Why do you wanta know?' Benton countered.

'I can't stick around here. They'll

throw me back behind bars if they catch me.'

'Then head for other parts. You can't ride with me.' Benton spurred his horse.

'I got caught trying to bust you out of jail,' Clinton protested. 'I work for Vince Parker, and he ordered me to hit the jail. So maybe Dunne will let me join your gang.'

'You better check with Parker. He might have other work for you.'

'I won't be any use to him now,' Clinton protested. 'I'm wanted by the law. He'll tell me to get lost.'

'Go and see him anyway.' Benton kicked his horse into greater effort. 'You'll likely get yourself killed if you stick around with me.'

Clinton reined in and watched Benton disappear into the night. Patton had angled off in a different direction as soon as he was clear of town and was disappearing in an eastward direction. Clinton listened to the fading hoof beats of Benton's horse as he gave thought to his future. It looked like he would have to quit Cedar Creek. The law would want him for his attack on the jail. But he could not leave without money, and Parker owed him for trying to bust Hussey loose. He swung his horse and rode back to town. With money in his pocket he could lose himself in the West and start a new life somewhere. He rode at a walk, and avoided the main street when he reached it. He headed for the back lots behind the Black Ace saloon and dismounted in the shadows.

The town seemed quiet. Clinton checked his gun; Parker might turn awkward because the attack on the jail had failed. He stole through the night to the rear door of the saloon only to discover it was locked. There were no lights anywhere. He entered the alley beside the saloon; lamplight was showing in a side window. Clinton went forward and peered through the dusty glass. He saw Peck, the undertaker, inside the bar room, and cold horror stabbed through him when he recognized the two motionless figures that were lying on the floor. Montell and Brazos — both dead!

Clinton moved away from the window, his nerves jangling. The new sheriff must have killed them, and now he knew what he could expect. He heard a noise in the street and sneaked along the alley to the boardwalk. The undertaker's assistant was pushing a hand cart, and stopped outside the saloon. Clinton waited in the shadows while the bodies of Montell, Brazos, and the bartender were carried out of the saloon and deposited on the cart. The lights in the saloon were extinguished, and then Peck and his assistant wheeled the hand cart off in the direction of the town mortuary. Clinton watched them depart, enveloped by a sense of loneliness.

Where was Vince Parker? Clinton stood lost in speculation. Perhaps Parker was dead also! But Parker never took any risks. He always paid others to do the dirty work, remaining in the clear no matter what happened. Clinton reached for his pistol. He needed money, and if Parker wasn't around to give him some then he was prepared to help himself.

He went to the batwings and eased silently into the darkened saloon. Silence pressed in around him and he made his way to the bar and helped himself to a much needed drink of whiskey. He moved stealthily along the back bar, feeling his way carefully, and found the metal box in which the bartender put the bar takings. The box was more than half filled with paper money and coins, and Clinton wasted no time in transferring the cash to his pockets. He moved unerringly through the darkness to Parker's office, and risked lighting a lamp.

The first thing he saw when lamp-light filled the office was the big safe in the corner standing open. Clinton knew from experience that the safe was always loaded with cash, for Parker did not believe in banks. Now it was bare.

He helped himself to another drink of whiskey while he considered. It looked like Parker had lit out fast. Perhaps he had made himself scarce because the jail break had failed. Clinton knew Parker had bought Big D. He unlocked the back door and went out to the barn where Parker stabled his horse. The animal was not in its stall. Clinton went back into the office.

He suspected that the law would be out in force to look for escaped prisoners, and settled down in the office to await sunup, whiling away the time with thoughts of his future while drinking copiously from Parker's private store of good whiskey.

★ ★ ★

Benton rode unerringly through the night. When they parted at the scene of the ambush, Buck Dunne had instructed Benton to rendezvous at the Diamond O ranch, and he hoped the gang boss was still there. He pushed his horse unmercifully. He did not want to lose contact with Dunne at this time because their cache of the proceeds from several bank robberies was hidden near their main hideout. If Dunne got his hands on the dough and took off alone, Benton knew his chances of getting a share of their ill-gotten haul would become non-existent.

He slowed his headlong pace before riding within earshot of Diamond O, and left the trail to circle the ranch house warily. When he saw Dunne's horse in the corral he grinned in relief. Skirting the yard, he reached the back of the house. A light was showing in the kitchen window. He dismounted, trailed his reins, and peered through the kitchen window. Shock speared through him when he saw Dunne lying on the floor. A woman was seated at the kitchen table, holding a rifle with its muzzle covering the fallen gang boss.

Benton's first reaction was to rush into the kitchen, but if the woman had shot Dunne then he would have to take it easy or he could wind up beside his boss. Tense moments passed as he considered the situation. He wondered if there was a crew on the cow spread, but discounted the thought because they would have rushed to the house upon hearing a shot. Mulling over the situation, he decided that an open approach might disarm the girl, and rapped on the door with bunched knuckles. He saw Sue jerk at the sound and swing the rifle to cover the door.

'Hello in the kitchen,' Benton called. 'I've been sent from town to check on you. Is everything OK? I thought I heard a shot as I came up.'

'Who's there?' Sue responded.

'I'm Hoagy Benton, ma'am. Doc Errol asked me to look in on you.'

Relief filled Sue when she heard the doctor's name mentioned. 'You can come in,' she said. 'The door is unlocked.'

Benton entered. He paused on the threshold and gazed at the levelled rifle.

'I don't blame you for being careful,'

he said, 'but you don't need a gun against me. What happened here? Who is that on the floor? Is he dead?'

'That's Buck Dunne, the outlaw,' Sue replied. She explained the incidents that had occurred at the ranch. 'He killed my brother in cold blood yesterday afternoon before he rode away, but he returned a while ago. I shot him when he tried to grab my rifle.'

'Can I take a look at him?' Benton demanded.

'Sure. And if he's dead perhaps you will get him out of here.'

Benton went to Dunne's side and bent over the outlaw. He was relieved to discover that Dunne was still alive despite the amount of blood staining his clothes. Benton discovered a bullet wound in Dunne's left side which no longer leaked blood. Dunne opened his eyes at that moment, and Benton realized the gang boss had not been unconscious. Dunne winked and closed his eyes.

'He ain't dead, Miss.' Benton looked up at Sue to discover the muzzle of the rifle gaping at him. 'I could bandage him if you like, and then take him back to town and jail him.'

'If he isn't dead then stand clear and I'll kill him,' Sue replied tensely. 'He murdered my brother in cold blood, and deserves to die.'

'There's no need for that.' Benton stood up and spread his hands. 'It looks to me like he's about ready to cash his chips,' he bluffed. 'I'll get him out of here — put him in the barn until he's gone.'

Sue heaved a ragged sigh. 'Please do that,' she agreed.

Benton picked up Dunne and carried him out of the kitchen. He staggered across to the barn and made Dunne comfortable on a pile of straw. He struck a match, located a lantern, and filled the barn with dim yellow light. Thankful to be away from the menace of Sue's rifle, he returned to Dunne and found the gang boss sitting up and grinning tensely at him.

'How did you get out of jail?' Dunne asked. 'I was coming back there later to bust you out. That gal damned near did for me. I must have laid there more than an hour, playing possum. If I'd have moved a finger she would have plugged me again for sure.'

'Are you bad hurt?' Benton asked.

'It feels like I've got a busted rib. But I'm still breathing so it can't be serious.'

'The girl thinks you are dying,' Benton said, 'so if she comes in here you better go on playing possum. She sure wants to see you dead.'

'My horse is in the corral,' Dunne said wearily. 'Fetch it for me and I'll ride on to Big D. Vince Parker has gone there. You grab that gal and bring her to me. I'll settle her hash! Before you leave here you can kill her father. He's lying wounded in a bedroom.'

'OK.' Benton nodded. 'You want the gal in one piece, huh?'

'That's what I said. Were you chased out of town?'

'No. I checked my back trail more than once. That guy, Frank Blaine, is wearing the sheriff's badge now, and he's a real handful! Parker sent several men to take care of him and he shot the hell out of them. They couldn't bust open the jail, and finally gave up.'

'Do you figure Blaine might trail along in this direction?' Dunne asked. 'He was living here after that big showdown last month. I should have looked him up when I had the chance. I want you to stay on here, Hoagy, until a couple of hours after sunup. If Blaine shows up, get the drop on him and bring him to Big D. I want to kill him. He's been on my trail for some time and I want to be rid of him.'

Benton nodded and went to fetch Dunne's horse. Dunne grunted in pain when he swung into the saddle, but his wound did not inconvenience him. He rode out for Big D. Benton watched him disappear out of sight before returning to the house. Sue was still sitting in the kitchen, although she had put aside the rifle. Benton eyed the weapon. He stood in the doorway, his hands down at his sides.

'He's gone, Miss,' he said. 'Just cashed in his chips. He is dead as a doornail! Shall I bury him out back?'

'No. Take him into town, if you are going back there.'

'I promised to report back to Doc Errol, so I will be heading that way shortly.'

Sue lost the last shreds of her suspicion. She got to her feet, leaving the rifle lying on the table. 'Can I get you something to eat?' she asked.

'It is getting close to breakfast time,' Benton replied, 'and I could sure do with a bite.'

'I'll cook you breakfast.' Sue stirred herself. She put a big pan on the stove.

'Doc said your pa was bad hurt in that shoot-out last month,' Benton observed. 'How is he doing now?'

Sue suppressed a sigh. 'He's an old man and his recovery is slow,' she replied.

'And Buck Dunne killed your brother yesterday?'

'Billy is still lying where Dunne dropped him — at the side of the porch.'

Benton sat down at the table. Dawn was not far off, and, when he began to eat the breakfast Sue had prepared for him he saw the first rays of sunlight at the kitchen window. While he ate, Benton considered Dunne's instructions. It did not occur to him to disobey his orders. He would wait a couple of hours after sunup to see if a posse was coming out from the town, and if all was well he would kill Chuck Ormond and then take the girl to Big D to whatever fate awaited her there.

10

Hilt was gaunt when he sighted Diamond O. He spotted smoke rising from the kitchen chimney of the ranch house, and the sight of it reminded him that he was ravenously hungry. He glanced at the sky; the sun was well clear of the horizon. His injured leg was paining him, and he would not be sorry to quit travelling for a few days. He wondered how Sue was coping with her grief. The death of her brother Billy must have been a terrific blow, and as he continued, he reaffirmed his vow to kill Buck Dunne.

He made a wide circuit of the ranch buildings, staying well out to maintain the surprise of his arrival. With Buck Dunne in the locality he could not afford to underestimate the outlaw. When he saw no sign of life on the ranch he halted the buggy behind the cook shack over by the corral. He dismounted, picked up the crutch, and stomped across the yard toward the nearest front corner of the ranch house. A playful breeze caused dust devils to whirl and race across the open stretch of ground. Hilt made his way to the rear of the building, impatient now to see Sue.

The kitchen door was not locked. He pushed it wide and a smell of freshly cooked food wafted tantalizingly across his nostrils. He propped his crutch against the door jamb and stepped over the threshold into the kitchen, favouring his right leg and calling Sue's name as he did so. He paused when he saw Sue sitting at the table with a rifle before her.

'Hello, Sue!' Hilt greeted. He narrowed his eyes because the kitchen was gloomy, and advanced two steps into the room before he noticed that Sue's wrists were bound together. He halted, his right hand dropping to the butt of his holstered pistol.

At that instant the open door was slammed with considerable force. Hilt spun around, caught a glimpse of a dark figure lunging at him, and clawed out his gun. Such was his speed that he was cocking the weapon with his thumb when his attacker hit him on the head with the barrel of a Colt .45. Pain blossomed in Hilt's skull. He felt blood begin to stream down his face from a gash on his forehead. His pistol was snatched from his hand and he lifted his left arm to shield his head from a second blow.

Benton's Colt swung back before descending again with terrific force. The obdurate metal made a second contact with Hilt's head and he pitched headlong to the floor as total darkness enveloped him. He felt as if he were falling into a deep well. His skull seemed to explode, and a flashing light, as brilliant as the sun, flared behind his eyes. Then the pain receded with his senses and he knew no more . . .

Hoagy Benton stood over Hilt's inert

body, pistol raised for yet another blow, but the new sheriff was unconscious, and Hoagy straightened with a grin. He looked across at Sue, bound hand and foot at the table.

'This must be my lucky day,' he observed. 'All the trouble they had last night trying to kill this guy, and he walked in here this morning as large as life and obliged me by presenting his head for his comeuppance like a lamb coming to the slaughter. I can't wait to see Dunne's face when I take this galoot to Big D.'

'Who are you?' Sue demanded. She had been plunged into a fresh nightmare from the moment Benton finished eating the breakfast she had cooked for him. He had risen from the table and seized her — bound her, and dumped her on a chair. For two hours he had lounged around the kitchen, apparently waiting for someone to arrive or something to happen, and Hilt, of all people, had walked in. She gazed at Hilt's motionless figure lying on the floor and was horrified by the sight of blood streaming from his head.

'It doesn't matter who I am,' Benton responded. 'We're gonna leave here shortly, and you better behave or it'll be worse for you.'

He examined Hilt before tying the new sheriff's wrists behind his back.

'I'm not going anywhere,' Sue protested. 'I can't leave my father here alone! He was badly wounded and needs a lot of attention.'

'You can quit worrying about your father,' Benton said. 'I'll take care of him before we leave.'

'What do you mean?' Horror filled Sue as she gazed at Benton's hard face.

'I got my orders. Just stay quiet and you won't get hurt. It's got nothing to do with me what happens to you when we get to Buck Dunne. He's the boss, and what he says goes.'

Benton left the kitchen and Sue listened intently when she heard his boots sounding on the stairs. Fear for her father rose in her mind and she struggled against her bonds but failed to make any impression on them. She heard Benton go into her father's bedroom. The silence that followed was agonizing, and she sat tense and worried until she heard Benton descending the stairs moments later.

'Have you harmed my father?' Sue asked when Benton reappeared in the doorway.

'Now why would I want to harm a wounded man?' Benton grinned. 'What do you take me for? I'll get a couple of horses ready and we'll ride to Big D.'

'Why take me there?' Sue demanded.

'Wait and find out.' Benton went to Hilt's side and checked him. 'He's coming round. He'll have the mother of all headaches when he wakes up. I'll put him in that buggy he came in, and you can drive him.'

Sue was greatly afraid that Benton had harmed her father. She struggled to free her wrists when Benton left the kitchen to fetch the buggy, but was still tightly bound when he returned. Hilt was stirring on the floor, but his eyes were closed. Benton shook Hilt until he opened his eyes. Hilt's face was pale. Blood had run down his face, giving him a gory mask.

'We're going for a ride,' Benton said. 'Don't give me any trouble or you'll be mighty sorry. Do I make myself clear?'

Hilt looked around wearily, trying to regain his scattered wits. His head ached as if it had been kicked by a mule. He frowned when he saw Sue seated at the table, her hands and feet bound. He looked at Benton, recognized the grinning outlaw, and his memory returned.

He tried to lift a hand to his aching head and discovered that he was bound tightly.

'You've made a big mistake by sticking around the county after getting out of jail,' Hilt told Benton. 'What are you doing here, anyway?'

'He's one of Buck Dunne's gang,' Sue said harshly. 'Dunne was here again earlier, Hilt. I shot him but he isn't dead. He's gone to Big D.'

'Quit talking,' Benton cut in. 'I'm taking you to Big D, Blaine, and it will be the end of the trail for you — Dunne wants the pleasure of killing you. Now shut up. Get on your feet, mister, and we'll make tracks.'

Hilt's senses spun and he had difficulty rising, but he finally made it and stood unsteadily, favouring his right leg.

'You ain't looking so tough now,' Benton observed. 'Come on, the buggy is outside.' He pushed Hilt toward the kitchen door and they went out into the early morning sunlight. 'I'll be back for you in a minute, girlie,' he promised Sue.

Hilt climbed into the buggy under the menace of Benton's gun and was tied to the seat. He tried to undo his bonds when Benton returned to the kitchen for Sue, but could not loosen the obdurate knots in the rope. Sue emerged from the kitchen and climbed into the buggy. Benton had untied her.

She looked at Hilt, her blue eyes wide and filled with shock. There was a faint bruise on her left cheek and a smear of blood around her swollen lips. Hilt noted that her hands were trembling as she took up the reins.

'Did Benton strike you, Sue?' Hilt demanded.

'Shuddup!' Benton swung into his saddle and rode in beside the buggy. 'OK,' he said in a clipped tone. 'You know where Big D is so get moving. And bear in mind that I'll be watching the pair of you every inch of the way. Don't try anything, mister, because Dunne will be disappointed if you're dead on arrival.'

Sue took up the whip, cracked it, and the horse moved out. Hilt closed his eyes, his thoughts moving fast. It was ironic that he had spent months hunting Buck Dunne, and now here he was being delivered to the outlaw like a sack of potatoes. He glanced over his shoulder. Benton was riding behind and to the left of the buggy. He was holding a pistol in his right hand and the weapon was covering Hilt.

The nagging pain in Hilt's right leg was countered by the crushing agony in his head. His brain felt as if it were bruised, and he had difficulty in thinking straight, but he knew he had to get free of his bonds and overpower Benton before they reached Big D. If Buck Dunne was at the ranch to receive him as a prisoner then his time was running out: Dunne would surely kill him out of hand. He glanced at Sue. The girl looked as if she was living in a nightmare. Her teeth were clenched and she gripped the reins, following the trail as if her mind was elsewhere.

Hilt was angry with himself for walking into trouble at Diamond O and getting caught so easily. He tested the rope binding his wrists and realized that he would never be able to undo the knots without help. Again he glanced at Sue, and decided that she could not help him. So it was up to him to get them out of the mess they were in. He tried to relax, to wait for the moment when the slightest chance might come his way, for when it came, as he knew it would if he remained vigilant, he would have to grab it with both hands. He smiled grimly as he considered that he was not dead yet, and while there was life there was hope.

'How far is it to Big D?' Hilt asked Sue.

The girl started as if her face had been slapped. She looked at him for a moment, considering his question, and then drew a deep breath. 'Ten miles,' she said tonelessly.

They continued, the horse cantering easily. Hilt looked around. The range was devoid of other human life, and he knew there was no help for them anywhere. He glanced at Benton again, and saw that the outlaw was highly alert . . .

★ ★ ★

Clinton fell asleep some time during the night and did not awaken until after the sun rose. He had put his feet up on the desk in Parker's office, and his left foot fell to the floor and brought him back to reality. He started up, and cursed when he realized that the sun was well above the horizon. He finished off the whiskey in the bottle on the desk and hurried out back to his horse. It was time to made tracks.

He cleared town without incident and hit the trail for Big D, which was situated beyond Diamond O and off to the north-east. He rode fast, wanting to get away from the area of the town in case a posse had turned out for the escaped prisoners. He spotted the wheels of a buggy on the trail and figured that the doctor was doing his rounds, until he recalled that the new sheriff had been using a buggy because of a leg wound. He kept an eye on the fresh wheel tracks because they were going in his direction.

When he sighted Diamond O he saw

that the buggy had turned into the ranch yard, and spotted where it had left again soon afterward. He frowned when he wondered if Frank Blaine was heading for Big D, and put his horse into a gallop. An hour later he topped a rise, and then swung his horse about quickly and rode off the skyline, for he had spotted the buggy only a few yards ahead. More, he recognized Benton riding behind the buggy, and the outlaw was holding a gun. He moved forward for another look, and saw that Sue was driving the buggy and the new sheriff was seated beside the girl, his hands tied tightly behind his back.

Clinton dropped back. So what was going on? Benton had obviously captured the prisoner and was taking him to Big D. Clinton decided to follow and check out the situation.

Hilt kept Benton under covert observation as they continued to Big D. Once he thought he heard the sound of a horse close on their back trail, and Benton must have heard it also for his attention was momentarily diverted from the buggy. Sue had obviously been watching for at that moment she slid her left hand around Hilt and fumbled with the knots holding him. He stiffened, and sat stock-still with hope blossoming in his mind. Was this the break he had been hoping for? He held his breath, hoping Benton was becoming less alert. When he felt the knot on his right wrist slacken a fraction he took a deep breath, twisted his hand, and it slid free of the rope.

Hilt held his hands as if they were still bound tightly, and risked a glance at Benton over his left shoulder. The outlaw had twisted in his saddle and was studying their back trail.

'Did you hear something?' Benton demanded. He looked around again, his sharp gaze sweeping across the undulating range. 'Get a move on. We're wasting time. Crack the whip, gal, and make that horse run.'

Sue obeyed and the buggy started rolling again. Hilt kept his hands together behind his back, hoping that Benton would not check his bonds. He watched the outlaw from a corner of his eye, waiting and hoping for an opportunity to grab the initiative from him.

Benton did not seem to be so alert. He allowed his pistol to rest on his right thigh as he rode. Hilt noticed that the pistol was not cocked.

Hilt glanced at Sue. She had a fixed smile on her face, but desperation shone in her blue eyes. She exchanged glances with Hilt, and nodded slightly in the direction of Benton, just a couple of feet to the left side of the buggy. Hilt frowned, wondering what was in her mind. She lifted the whip a fraction as if intending to crack it over the horse, but tilted it slightly in Benton's direction, and Hilt wondered what she intended.

'You're in my way, so lean forward a little,' she said in a half-whisper.

'Cut out the gab,' Benton rasped.

Hilt leaned forward as if his senses were failing, but steeled himself to follow up whatever Sue was planning.

He saw her glance again at Benton, and then she twisted in her seat and struck at the outlaw with the long lash. Hilt ducked and the lash whipped over his head with barely an inch to spare. He glanced around at Benton; he saw that the lash was perfectly timed. It coiled around Benton's gun wrist like a black snake. Sue jerked the whip savagely, pulling Benton's arm away from his side. His pistol flipped out of his hand as the lash bit into his flesh. Hilt, watching closely, sprang up and made a desperate grab at the gun as it whirled in his direction.

The barrel of the pistol struck Hilt's outstretched palm and his long fingers closed around it. He heard Benton's cry of pain. Reversing the weapon, he grasped the butt and cocked the weapon. Benton was pulling on the whip, trying to wrest it from Sue's grasp, and she released it suddenly.

Hilt swung the pistol to cover Benton. The outlaw froze in his saddle, shocked by the sudden turn of events.

'It looks like the boot is now on the other foot, Benton,' Hilt said harshly. 'Get down from your horse and stand still.'

Benton dismounted quickly. Hilt got out of the buggy, the pistol levelled.

'Please, Hilt, let's hurry back to Diamond O,' Sue called anxiously. 'I think Benton killed my pa before we left. He said Dunne told him to do it.'

'What about it, Benton?' Hilt demanded. 'Did you kill Chuck Ormond?'

'Hell, no, I didn't!' Benton blustered. 'What do you take me for? I wouldn't kill an injured man.'

'Get your hands up above your shoulders, I want to search you,' Hilt commanded, and Benton's hands shot above his head.

'I don't have another weapon on me,' Benton protested. 'You've got me fair and square. I give in.'

Hilt searched Benton. The man was unarmed. Hilt motioned to Sue.

'Tie him with that rope, Sue. We'll take him back with us. It's only a few miles. Then I'll have to go on to Big D. If I get a good break now I can finish this trouble today.'

Benton was tied in the buggy. Sue picked up her whip and resumed her seat in the vehicle. Hilt climbed into Benton's saddle. Sue cracked the whip and swung the buggy around, then drove the horse back to Diamond O. Hilt gritted his teeth against the pain in his right thigh as he followed closely. He would rather have been riding in the opposite direction, but Sue came first in his estimation, and he urged the horse on.

Clinton sat behind a crest and watched the tables being turned on Benton. He was tempted to step in and help the outlaw, but had too much respect for the new sheriff. He waited until the buggy had gone from sight and then regained his saddle and set off fast for Big D. An hour later he rode into the ranch yard and hammered toward the house. Vince Parker appeared on the porch, attracted by the sound of hoof beats, and Buck Dunne emerged from the doorway, a gun in his hand. The outlaw's shirt was open to the waist and revealed a thick bandage wrapped around his lower ribs.

'What's going on?' Dunne demanded. 'What's your all-fired hurry?'

Clinton explained. Before he was halfway through his account, Dunne was moving off to the corral.

'Come on, Parker,' he rasped. 'That damn Blaine is proving a hard nut to crack. He's been looking for me for a long time, and I reckon it is about time he found me. I'll send him to join his brother. Let's ride to Diamond O.'

Parker wanted to cry off, but he knew better than to cross Dunne.

'You come too, Clinton,' he ordered, 'and get Ed Brown from the corral. He'll be a good man to have along.'

They saddled up and rode out fast for Diamond O. Despite the wound he had received, Buck Dunne set the pace.

When Sue swung into the Diamond O yard she stopped the horse in front of the porch, jumped down, and ran to the house. Hilt dismounted and checked Benton's bonds.

'You'd better be sitting here when I come back for you,' Hilt warned, and hurried into the house after Sue.

Hilt ascended the stairs to the bedrooms and hastened into Chuck Ormond's room. Sue was bending over her father's still figure on the bed. Hilt saw fresh blood on the bed clothes and a cold hand seemed to squeeze icy fingers around his heart.

'Is he dead?' he demanded.

Sue was crying. Her hands shook as she examined her father. Hilt went to her side. He took hold of Chuck Ormond's right wrist and felt for a pulse. The rancher was unconscious and scarcely breathing.

'He is alive,' Hilt said sharply.

Sue unfastened her father's shirt. Hilt saw a knife wound in Chuck's chest.

'Benton stabbed him,' he said harshly. 'Get a bowl of water, Sue, and we'll clean him up.'

Sue ran from the room. Hilt went to the window and looked down at the buggy. Benton was sitting motionless on the seat, his wrists bound behind his back. He was trying to free himself. Hilt banged on the window and, when Benton looked up guiltily, Hilt lifted a warning finger. Benton subsided, but a moment later he resumed his efforts to get free. Sue returned with water and bandages. Hilt watched her as she treated her father.

'He's tough like whang leather,' Hilt observed when Sue had finished her ministrations. 'The knife wound is high in the chest and looks like it missed his vital spots. I reckon he'll pull through OK, but he'll need the doctor. I'll stay here and watch him while you fetch Doc Errol. I daren't leave you here, Sue, in case Dunne turns up again.'

'I'll go, and I'll be as quick as I can,' Sue replied.

She took a long look at her father's craggy face and then ran from the room. Moments later, Hilt heard a

255

horse racing across the yard. He heaved a sigh and went down to the porch. Sue was already in the distance, galloping toward the town, He turned his attention to the sullen-faced Benton.

'You stuck a knife in Chuck Ormond,' he accused.

'Yeah, I can't deny it,' Benton said penitently. 'But I didn't mean to kill him. He ain't dead is he? It looks like that gal is on her way to fetch the doctor. For Gawd's sake say he ain't dead!'

'He's still alive,' Hilt replied. 'But I reckon they'll hang you anyway, when you come to trial.'

Hilt examined Benton's bonds. They were still tight. Benton would not be able to get free without help. Hilt looked around. The ranch was silent and still. He crossed to the end of the porch and looked down at the two bodies lying there. Billy Ormond and John Fletcher; killed by Buck Dunne. A pang of impatience struck through him. How many more men would die before

Dunne reached the end of his trail? He was desperate to get after the outlaw for he knew this was the chance he had been waiting for and he should strike while the opportunity existed. But he could not leave Chuck Ormond alone.

The unmistakable thud of a bullet striking the front wall of the house close to his left shoulder had Hilt jumping for the open doorway at his side, and he gained cover before the crash of the rifle that fired the shot reached his ears. He drew his pistol and ran to a window to look for the rifleman, and ducked when a fusillade of shots hammered furiously. Half a dozen bullets crashed into the front of the house like hailstones. Glass tinkled from the windows; gun echoes smashed the silence. ✗

Hilt moved quickly despite the ache in his leg. He pressed against the wall beside a broken window and peered out, gun raised; his finger was steady on the trigger. He risked a look through the window and a bullet snarled at him

257

so close to his left cheek that he imagined he felt the heat of it. He ducked back into cover, but not before he saw four riders coming around the corral, firing rapidly as they galloped toward the house. He risked another quick look, and recognized Buck Dunne slightly in the lead, shooting rapidly and putting his slugs through the window where Hilt was positioned.

Wild elation filled Hilt. After months of trailing and chasing the outlaw, Dunne was coming for him. He moved to the doorway, filled with deadly determination. The end of his man hunt was at hand. He or Dunne, or both of them, would die in this confrontation. At long last, his brother Thad would be avenged: a twist of fate had brought the killer within range of his lethal gun.

The four riders came into the yard and raised dust as they hammered toward the house, shooting unrestrainedly. Hilt peered from the doorway as slugs splintered the woodwork. He had Buck Dunne in his sights now and would not be denied. He saw one of the riders peel off to the right and disappear around the corner of the house, evidently making for the kitchen door. Hilt held his fire and waited. He would get only one chance to kill Dunne and did not intend to make any mistakes.

The trio reached the house, guns blazing as they riddled the porch and the windows to cow resistance. Hilt recognized another of the riders as Vince Parker, the saloon man; the third man was Clinton. Hilt thrust his pistol forward, drew a bead on Parker, and squeezed his trigger. Gun smoke blew back into his face. The pistol recoiled, and Parker whirled his horse away to the left, reeling in his saddle with blood spurting from his left shoulder.

Dunne rode up to the porch directly in front of the doorway, his reins in his teeth. He had a pistol in each hand, and fired them alternately. Clinton galloped past the open doorway, veered into the porch, and sprang from his saddle. Hilt shot Clinton in the chest as his boots hit the boards, and the man sprawled forward, his impetus taking him into the nearest window. Glass shattered and Clinton came to rest with his head and shoulders through the window frame.

Hilt's ears rang with the crash of the shooting. He stepped into the open doorway as Dunne reined in before it. Dunne lifted his Colts. Hilt drew a bead on the outlaw's chest. Dunne was snarling like a bear disturbed from its winter sleep. Hilt heard the sound of boots pounding bare boards somewhere in the back of the house and realized that the fourth attacker was closing in. But nothing could distract him from his vow to kill Buck Dunne. He squeezed his trigger, felt the familiar recoil of the weapon, and saw Dunne jerk under the impact of the heavy slug. The outlaw fired at the same instant. Hilt felt the terrific smash of a bullet striking him in the left side of his chest. Pain filled him. He dropped to his knees in the doorway as strength fled from his legs.

Dunne dropped one of his pistols.

Blood had spread across the outlaw's chest. His mouth was agape and blood bubbled from between his lips. He used two hands to try and bring his Colt into line with Hilt's figure. Hilt leaned his left shoulder against the door jamb. He felt suddenly weary, almost too exhausted to continue, but he took a fresh aim at Dunne and fired again. Dunne lost his balance as the second slug hit him. He was dead as he pitched sideways and fell out of his saddle. His right foot became trapped in the stirrup and the nervous horse took off at a gallop across the yard, dragging Dunne through the dust.

Hilt was mindful of the fourth man coming from the kitchen. He forced himself around to cover the door that gave access to the rear of the house. His eyes had trouble focusing and he squinted as he lifted his smoking gun. The door was thrust open and a man lunged into the big room. Hilt's Colt blasted. The man stopped as if he had run into the side of a barn. His gun fell from his hand and thudded on the floor. He dropped to his knees as if intent on saying his prayers, and then flopped forward on to his face and remained motionless.

Hilt cocked his gun and grasped the door to force himself to his feet. He could feel blood dribbling from his wound and pressed his left hand against his ribs where throbbing pain flared from the .45 slug nestling against a rib. He tucked his left elbow against the leaking wound and lurched out of the house to stagger across the porch. He looked for Buck Dunne. The outlaw gang boss was lying inertly in the dust some yards away.

Hilt maintained his balance by sheer force of will and went to where Dunne was lying. He passed the buggy, in which Benton was seated stock-still and helpless in his bonds, badly shocked by the shooting. The pain in Hilt's right thigh did not seem to hurt so much now. He reached Dunne and gazed down at the outlaw. Dunne had reached the end of his violent trail. His face was set in a snarl of defiance that would mark him until his flesh rotted from his bones.

Hilt heaved a long sigh and staggered to the porch. He dropped wearily into the rocker and closed his eyes, aware of a great sense of relief swelling inside him. He had killed the man who shot his brother. Now all he could do was await Sue's return with Doc Errol.

THE END

We do hope that you have enjoyed reading this large print book.

Did you know that all of our titles are available for purchase?

We publish a wide range of high quality large print books including:
Romances, Mysteries, Classics
General Fiction
Non Fiction and Westerns

Special interest titles available in large print are:
The Little Oxford Dictionary
Music Book, Song Book
Hymn Book, Service Book

Also available from us courtesy of Oxford University Press:
Young Readers' Dictionary
(large print edition)
Young Readers' Thesaurus
(large print edition)

For further information or a free brochure, please contact us at:
Ulverscroft Large Print Books Ltd.,
The Green, Bradgate Road, Anstey,
Leicester, LE7 7FU, England.
Tel: (00 44) **0116 236 4325**
Fax: (00 44) **0116 234 0205**

Rancher Cliff Sinclair offers the delighted homesteaders of Two Forks three dollars for each acre of their land. They accept this apparently generous offer, but Dalton is dubious. Only he and his friend Loren Steele refuse the offer, and his suspicions are confirmed when Cliff's hired gunslinger, Frank Kelley, kills Loren and runs Dalton out of town. As Dalton seeks vengeance, he and the speed of his gun hand will be tested to the limit.

OUTLAW QUEEN

Ethan Flagg

In Wyoming, an outlaw gang named the Starrbreakers causes mayhem. After every robbery the bandits vanish into the stronghold of the Big Horn Mountains through a gap known as the Hole in the Wall. The law authorities are powerless to hunt them down, so Special Agent Drew Henry is hired to infiltrate the gang in the guise of an escaped convict. Bullets will fly when he comes to town. When Henry takes on the Outlaw Queen can he break the Starrbreakers' stranglehold?